Jenny of the Tetons

KRISTIANA GREGORY

Jenny of the Tetons

Gulliver Books • Harcourt, Inc.

San Diego · New York London

Title page photo 1872 by William Henry Jackson. Left to right:
Beaver Dick, John, Anne Jane, Jenny holding William (she is days
away from delivering her fifth child, Elisabeth), Dick Junior on donkey.
Courtesy of American Heritage Center, University of Wyoming.

www.HarcourtBooks.com

First Gulliver Books paperbacks edition 2002

Gulliver Books is a trademark of Harcourt, Inc., registered in the
United States of America and/or other jurisdictions.

Library of Congress Cataloging-in-Publication Data
Gregory, Kristiana.
Jenny of the Tetons/Kristiana Gregory.
      p.   cm.
"Gulliver Books."
Summary: Orphaned by an Indian raid while traveling West with a wagon
train, fifteen-year-old Carrie Hill is befriended by the English trapper Beaver
Dick and taken to live with his Indian wife, Jenny, and their six children.
1. Leigh, Richard, d. 1899—Juvenile fiction.   [1. Leigh, Richard, d. 1899—
Fiction.   2. Frontier and pioneer life—Idaho—Teton Valley—Fiction.
3. Shoshoni Indians—Fiction.   4. Bannock Indians—Fiction.
5. Indians of North America—Fiction.]   I. Title.
PZ7.G8619Je   2002
[Fic]—dc21   2001039233
ISBN 0-15-216770-6

Text set in Granjon
Designed by Lori McThomas Buley

A C E G H F D B

For my parents,
honeymoon campers on Jenny Lake

The author wishes to acknowledge
the generous cooperation of research historian
Emmett D. Chisum, of the American Heritage Center
at the University of Wyoming, Laramie.

The Indian women are remarkable for their affection and fidelity to their husbands.

— GEORGE FREDERICK RUXTON,
Life in the Far West, 1849

The ravages of the Small Pox (which Swept off 400 men & Womin & children in perpopotion) has reduced this nation.... The cause or way those people took the Small Pox is uncertain, the most Probable, from Some other nation by means of a warparty.

—WILLIAM CLARK, 14 August 1804,
The Journals of Lewis and Clark

Jenny of the Tetons

Author's Note

When the Hayden Survey of 1872 explored northwestern Wyoming, an Englishman named Richard "Beaver Dick" Leigh led the explorers into the Teton Valley and Jackson Hole. Members of the survey team, among them William Henry Jackson, the first great photographer of the West, were so impressed by their guide and his Shoshone wife that they named Jenny Lake and Leigh Lake, at the base of the Tetons, for them. When this area became a national park, in 1929, Beaver Dick Lake was renamed String Lake.

Beaver Dick chronicled wilderness life through letters and journals, which he wrote phonetically with no punctuation. He and Jenny had six children in what was a primitive but happy life until tragedy struck. Each chapter of *Jenny of the Tetons* begins with an excerpt from Beaver Dick's journal. The story is told by fifteen-year-old Carrie Hill, a fictional pioneer girl who could easily have been Jenny's friend.

In my search for accuracy, I had the privilege of long conversations with American Indians from the Shoshone-Bannock tribe on the Fort Hall Reservation in Idaho. Because of their oral histories, they were able to describe what it was like in this area during the mid-1800s. Little is known about Jenny's early years, but it is thought she may have been orphaned by a warring tribe, possibly the Blackfeet. One legend says she married a French fur trapper at a young age (thirteen or fourteen) but was soon widowed.

Special thanks go to my newfound friends who patiently answered questions and explained traditions: Kaylene Buckskin for Shoshoni translations; Emma Dann, a Lemhi-Shoshone whose grandfather Chief Tendoy was Sacajawea's cousin; Clyde Hall, of Shoshone and Cree lineage, an attorney for the tribal courts and consultant for the David T. Vernon Museum of Indian Arts at Colter Bay Visitor Center in Jackson Hole; and Duane

Thompson, superintendent for the Bureau of Indian Affairs and great-grandson of Beaver Dick.

Kristiana Gregory
Pocatello, Idaho, 1987

Part One

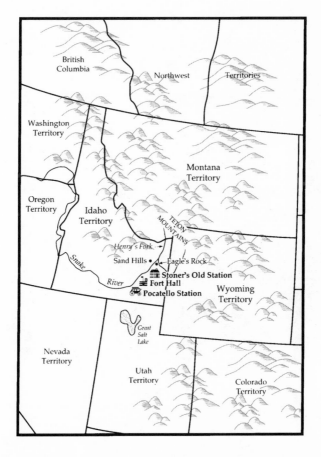

1875 Map of Fort Hall, Pocatello, and Henry's Fork Area

1

"nooned at poketela [Pocatello] stat[i]on then traveld . . .
to fort hall . . . dune some trading hear for our fall's
trap[p]ing and hunting"

24–25 July 1875

Our wagon train, what was left of it, pulled into Fort
Hall just after sundown. July heat smothered the
darkening desert. A cluster of tipis around the
outer walls only increased my terror.

"She's just a child, poor thing," a woman's voice
said. She was close to my face, looking by candle-
light at my bandage. A cool hand touched my
forehead as someone lifted me from the wagon
bed and carried me to a pallet inside the fortress.
Voices whispered.

"You're safe now," the woman said.

"Mother?" I tried to lift my head.

"Rest, my dear."

———

It was nearly a week before I could walk on my own. The sunlight almost blinded me when I stepped outside to the courtyard. It was noisy, with travelers shouting to one another as they carried crates or rolled huge wagon wheels through the gravel. Children sat in the shade, oiling harnesses. Yokes, cracked from dryness, were stacked near a carpenter's bench. Most emigrants rested just a day or two before continuing on the trail west to Oregon.

I recognized Mr. Hardy, one of our drivers, watering the mules. It looked like he'd be moving on soon, even though he was leaning on a crutch. Next to the corral was the open shed of the blacksmith, who was turning iron spikes in the fire. His beard was so long that he had tucked its tip into the belt at his waist. Log buildings lined the base of the walls; and high up on top, soldiers. Sun reflected off their coat buttons and the metal of their rifles.

Watching them walk back and forth made me feel safe, until I looked across the yard and saw the Indians. They were gathered around one of the cabins—trading, maybe. At least a dozen. I felt dizzy again.

"Carrie?"

I opened my eyes. Someone had tucked a quilt around me.

"Sweet child, can you hear me?" It was Mrs. Lander. She bent close enough to whisper. Her bonnet hid the men standing behind her.

I nodded.

"We're leaving first thing tomorrow, the rest of us are. Come with us, won't you, dear?" She squeezed my arm gently. "Your folks would've wanted it, I'm certain."

There was a stab in my stomach at the thought of returning to that prickly old trail, with babies crying all the time and dust turning to mud in my mouth. More weeks of coughing. More weeks of worrying about another ambush. I could still taste metal from the axle grease Mother had smeared on our lips.

Not too far back were the graves of my parents. Joey, Samuel, and baby Ivan were gone, too. To leave them behind would be worse than anything I could imagine. Worse even than what had put them there in the first place.

I turned my head to the wall.

"Still can't hardly get a word outta her." It was a man's voice outside the cabin wall. Sunlight speckled between the logs onto the quilt over my legs. "Fifteen's awful young to lose your whole family," he said.

"Well, she ain't gonna be happy here, Capt'n Putnam, not with ninety of your enlisted men trying to see through her skirts every blessed moment," said the voice I'd learned to recognize as Mr. Shilling's.

Mr. Shilling ran the trading post in the fort. Mrs. Lander told me he was licensed by the U.S. government, as long as he didn't sell alcohol to the Indians or ammunition if they were planning to go on the warpath. Guns for hunting, now—that was different. He could swap as many of their skins or blankets for guns as he wanted, just so long as they were shooting for food. But to me, an Indian with a rifle only meant some*thing* or some*body* was destined for buckshot.

"Way I see it, Capt'n, is Miss Hill can do one of three things. Stay here and cook hotcakes for your boys, mend their sleeves, and such." Shilling hawked up a mouthful of phlegm and ptooied into the dirt.

"Two, she can hitch up with Hardy's bunch for the promised land, which she don't seem likely to favor. Or"—he spit again—"there's the Englishman."

"Beaver Dick?"

"I wouldn't be a bit surprised, nossir, I would not, if the wife don't need an extra hand with all those young'uns."

Next morning in the early chill, I packed. It was the quickest thing I ever did: one gingham dress and an underskirt, my journal, and the thick tortoiseshell comb Mrs. Lander had rescued from my mother's hair. I held up Mother's tiny looking glass, but when I saw the jagged gash across my forehead I threw it into the fireplace, where it bounced among the ashes.

"Excuse me, Miss Carrie," said a figure in the doorway. "It's time."

I was immediately embarrassed, for Miles Alexander was by far the most sturdy man I'd ever enjoyed watching. He was the fort's main carpenter—older than I, and tall. For two weeks we'd been glancing at each other, and every time he had smiled, my neck had grown hot.

The Englishman waited outside the gates with three mules loaded high and two Appaloosas. His hair was red as rust, with a beard to match. Sweat stains on his hat and down the front of his vest reminded me of the heat ahead of us, two days' worth. Freckles and blue eyes. He winked as he handed me the reins to the smaller horse.

"This 'ere's Billy Button." He was rolling my bundle into a gray blanket that he tied to the back of the saddle. "I gave 'im to my little son, William, last spring. Up, Missie," he said with a lift to my boot heel. His accent was the same as my father's had been.

"Off and away with a yay dilly yay." And with a happy shout, he began whistling. The mules followed, slowly, as if they were considering another plan. A few minutes later we reached the Snake River, which would lead us north to Henry's Fork and my new home. The galloping of a horse behind us interrupted the whistler, and we both turned to see Miles Alexander leaning forward in his saddle, dust kicking up around him.

"You forgot this!" he yelled, pulling alongside Billy Button. The mirror I'd left for dead now sparkled in the sun as he slipped it into the big pocket on my riding skirt. Then he put his hand over mine.

"Come fall, I'll be working out of Sand Hills; that's the post just south of Dick's place." He took a long breath. "Carrie, I'd be honored if you'd let me call on you." Our legs swayed into each other as the horses continued forward. His eyes were very blue.

"The honor would be mine."

2

*"i wanted to take my famly along but my Wife wold
not consent she sade it wold be too mutch truble
packing every thing away from hear"*

Summer 1875

As we followed the Snake, I started to feel
scared. Tipis, at least twenty, were camped along
the riverbank where it was cool. Indians sat by the
low openings, facing the morning sun. Facing us.
The Englishman waved to them, and some waved
back.

"Shoshoni," he said. He slowed until we were
riding side by side. He waved again to a brave
standing by a little boy. Both wore calico shirts and
dungarees with red sashes around their waists.
The Englishman motioned with his hand and fingers, then opened his palm near my shoulder. The

16

Indian drew his hand in the air. They were talking to each other.

"My friends welcome you," Dick said. "You are wished good living."

Lucky thing my words stuck in my throat. I might have started a war. Indians wishing me a good life? They might be Beaver Dick's friends, but they would never be mine.

I was glad when their stick tents were behind us. We passed Grove City, where the only sound was the clinking of horseshoes in the livery stable. A big yellow dog woofed at us, then went back to the shade for his nap.

When the sun was overhead, we stopped by some willows where the river was high and gentle. Lunch was a quiet affair: boiled eggs from the fort, hardtack, and jerky. I couldn't figure out what to say to this man who sounded just like my father but looked like he'd never seen a school or a barber in his life. If he fell asleep, his clothes could probably walk him home without waking him.

"Drink up, Missie." He handed me a tin cup. He dipped his hat into the river, then dumped it over his head.

"You'll be a 'eck of a lot cooler if y'do the same." He shivered under another dousing. I lay on my stomach where the grass was wet and rolled my head into the water.

For a long while as we rode, my braid dripped down my back. He was right. I was cooler. Beaver Dick didn't exhaust himself with talk, so I was free to think. To remember my family. I lagged with the mules, so he couldn't see me cry.

I was only six years old when Father put us on a train in Grimsby, England, bound for the harbor of Liverpool. The Amazon *took sixty-three days to reach New Orleans, having lost three sails in a storm but none of her passengers. Mother said there were more than eight hundred Mormons on board, all on their way to the New World. My father was a doctor and a stiff Presbyterian. He didn't understand this new religion of Joseph Smith's, but he wanted his medicine to help America's settlers, whatever their beliefs. And he wanted to make a better life for us.*

From New Orleans we headed up the Mississippi on a paddleboat, which scared me because one side tilted down toward the water. I remember an old woman. She was trying to help her daughter, who lay among a pile of blankets on deck about to give birth. The old woman leaned over the railing to fill a bucket, but she fell in. Her daughter screamed, and some men shouted up to the wheelroom for the captain to stop.

"Hell, it's just a Mormon!" the captain yelled back. He wouldn't stop the boat. He just kept going.

Father delivered the baby just before we docked in Saint Louis. He held my mother and told us that cruelty such as the captain's was no one's right. Mormons bled the same color as everyone else.

"A good heart," Father said, "has no room for hatred."

Then he put us on a smaller boat for Hannibal, where we lived for seven years. A week after Ivan was born, we packed up again. This time our dream was to head for Oregon, along with Mr. Hardy and nine other families.

I know Father didn't plan on an early grave or expect that his daughter would be left alone with strangers in Idaho Territory.

Beaver Dick and I camped that night on the river next to the tumbled logs of Stoner's old station. The mosquitoes were wild until our fire smoked them out. I curled in my blanket facing the flames and didn't wake until I smelled the Englishman's coffee at dawn. We nooned at the waterfalls of Eagle's Rock. High above us, the birds watched from their nests.

"Few more hours, 'ome," he said, lifting himself into his saddle. I had gotten good at mounting without his help.

"Does she, well, will she . . ." I wasn't sure what I wanted to ask. "Will your wife like me?"

He turned to look back at me. His beard moved up in a smile. "She will, Missie."

When the Snake headed east, we kept north on Henry's Fork. Soon I could see a cabin sitting beyond a wide stream. Beaver Dick stood in his stirrups and waved his arm like a flag to the figures moving excitedly toward us.

When we were close enough to see their faces, a chill ran through me. I hadn't been prepared for what awaited me. Now, more than ever, I would need to consider Father's words.

3

*"the flys and misqutos ad beene so bad that i scarcly
knew my owne horses and catle when i got home my
Wife and childrun ad sufred more than death thay ad
to keep Big smokes all day and half the nights to
keep the varmant of [off] the stock"*

July 1875

An Indian woman stood at the edge of the stream.
In her arms she held a large papoose. The child
was wrapped tight in buckskin, with a beaded
canopy shading its head.

Four other children splashed into the stream toward us, two hound dogs leading the way.

"Oppah, Oppah!" they cried.

The water lapped at the horses' stomachs as we
waded across. My boots were soaked to the ankle
before I thought to lift them out of the stirrups.

"Did you bring candy, Oppah?" called a pretty
girl about nine years old. Her black hair fell
straight below her shoulders. She was barefoot,

21

and like her mother, she wore a calico dress. The girl and her brothers were half-breeds. I felt dizzy again and shoved my legs back into the water so I wouldn't embarrass myself by fainting. It also cooled my temper.

That rotten Mr. Shilling. He said the English-man's wife was one of the finest women he ever did meet. Handsome children and all that fancy talk. He failed to mention that she was an Indian. My parents would be kicking the dirt from their graves if they knew I was living with a native and a mountain man, no school or church in sight. Tonight in the dark, when everyone was asleep, I would run away.

Before I had the chance to feel sorry for myself, Beaver Dick began making the introductions.

"Dick Junior is our eldest," he said about the boy untying the mule packs. He was as big as my brother Samuel—about eleven, I guessed.

"John 'ere, now 'e knows more about sage 'ens than I do." John was wriggling his toes in the dirt, like little brown mice digging for cover. "Got you a birthday surprise, son."

Beaver Dick hefted up the youngest boy and

caught him midair. "You and William's pony are old friends," he said with an eye my way, "so this 'ere's William. Too big for my shoulders anymore." William looked like the others, but his hair was blond like mine, and he had his dad's blue eyes. He was the same size as my brother Joey, and suddenly I felt mad. Why weren't *they* here with me, instead of strangers? It wasn't fair.

"Anne Jane." Dick rested his hand on her dark head. "You've got yourself a new friend, m'daughter." She and her brothers looked at me with polite curiosity, then cast their eyes down.

Dick put his arm around the woman and faced me. "Jenny, this 'ere's Miss 'ill, Carrie 'ill, an orphan girl, to 'elp you out like y' asked for." He leaned down to kiss the child in her arms. "'Ello, Elisabeth. 'Ow 'bout a dance?" He waved the mosquitoes away from her face.

Jenny leaned the cradleboard against a tree and started toward me. I couldn't read her face, and for a moment I was afraid. Maybe she was mad. Maybe Indians didn't like strangers moving in unannounced.

She stopped a couple of feet in front of me and

held out her hands. When I put mine in hers, she smiled.

"Carrie Hill, welcome."

The doorway was low, so I stooped to enter. It was dark except for the afternoon sun slanting in one of the windows. A fire under a kettle filled the room with heavy smoke. Jenny led me to a corner, where she unrolled a brown fur large enough to fit a buffalo. Junior laid my bundle on it, and William handed me a reed whistle.

I realized this was home.

4

"dick [Junior] returned with his rideng sadle coverd with malard and teele Ducks"

August 1875

"Have yourself a seat, Missie," Dick said.

I looked for a chair, but then noticed that the children were sitting cross-legged on the plank floor. Jenny dipped a long spoon into the kettle, filled a wooden bowl, and handed it to me. I tried to sit, too, but my boots were too stiff. I wobbled a bit and suddenly crashed down next to Anne Jane. Stew splashed everywhere. The bowl landed upside down on my knee.

"Oh, ma'am, I'm sorry!" I wanted to die. For a second I thought Jenny would hit me with her spoon. Instead, her shoulders started moving, and I could see she was laughing.

Now the children giggled. They're making fun of me, I thought. My clothes are soaked with mush, my boots have shrunk on my feet, and these dreadful people think it's funny. Tears were choking my throat. I tried to get up to run outside, but I was stuck.

"Ere y' go, Missie, up." Dick held my shoulders and lifted me high enough for my legs to straighten; then he put his face down by mine. He grinned.

"Y' just did Stumpy and Nig a big favor." He nodded toward the hound dogs, who were happily lapping up the mess. Their tails wagged. It was obvious that eating spilled stew was one of their jobs, for now the floor was clean except for little wet spots in the dust.

"I'll help you with your boots, Carrie," offered Anne Jane. So I eased myself back down and stuck my legs straight out. After a few heave-hos and no sight of my toes, Dick pulled a knife from his belt.

"Don't cut them off," I started to cry, but before the words were out, he had slit the leather from top to heel and opened the boots like books. To my shame he peeled my soggy leggings off, and now all of us stared at a pair of feet whiter than creamed potatoes. For several long moments, the only sound was the dogs' panting.

More than anything I wanted to cry. I wasn't used to feeling clumsy, especially in front of strangers. But suddenly I started to laugh, a deep laugh of relief that hadn't come out of me since Hannibal. When Dick threw the boots out the door, the dogs chased them like they were after scared raccoons.

Now we all laughed.

While I was getting used to bare legs under my skirt, Dick tossed his pack on a pallet against the wall. The pack was made of deerskin, folded like a giant envelope. The children immediately rushed over, jumping and wiggling.

"First, our birthday boy." Dick kneeled on the floor. "Come 'ere, son." He put a small pocket-knife in John's hand.

"Seven's about the perfect age for a boy to skin 'is own rockchuck, so 'ere y' go." At first John was speechless. Then he ran outside with a whoop.

One by one Dick handed out gifts. Jenny had unlaced the cradleboard, and I was surprised to see Elisabeth toddle across the room. She was at least two years old and quite chubby.

"Oppah," she said, lunging for her father's arm. "Oppah, Oppah."

"'Ello, jolly girl." He rolled his fist in a circle as if he were doing a magic trick, then opened his palm. Elisabeth grabbed the peppermint stick. "Mr. Shilling, this is from 'im. 'E says a baby without sweets is like a 'orse without feets!" Dick roared with laughter and lifted her over his head with a swoop into his arms. "Boo!" he said, his nose touching hers. She gave a happy shriek and grabbed his beard.

Anne Jane stood quietly by her mother's side. Dick winked at her and then curled Elisabeth into his arm. With his free hand he rummaged in his pack.

"Girl smart as you, Anne Jane, can't be without this." He held out a small, square package tied with string, which she opened slowly. "You're m'star, daughter."

"Al-isses Ad-ven-toors," she read. "Oppah, there are pictures, too."

"Adventures in Wonderland, m'girl. Now," he said to William. He tugged at the little boy's suspenders, then spun a tiny red top at his feet. "Make 'er dance, son."

After Dick settled a new black derby on Junior's head, he stood up. "The Queen 'as not been forgotten," he said with a bow toward Jenny. "Your beautiful eyes have new things to look at, thanks to Dr. Curtis of Philadelphia." He unwrapped a large oilskin parcel. Inside were several newspapers, a bolt of blue-checked gingham, silk handkerchiefs, and a magazine with a fancy city lady on the front.

"Harper's," Jenny said, reaching for the magazine. She was smiling. "Thank you, Ingabumbee."

Darkness soon moved into the valley. Dick leaned against the stone hearth and read aloud by the firelight from Anne Jane's new book. Jenny sat next to him, stitching beads onto a patch of leather, while the children listened quietly from their pallets. Even under the buffalo robe, I was shivering. My ears and face burned so hot it ached to keep my eyes open. I touched the gash on my forehead. It stung under my fingers and felt swollen. My plans for running away would have to wait. Dick's voice faded in and out as sleep washed over me.

Then Jenny's cool hand was on my face. She touched the gash with something damp that smelled faintly of mint. She began to sing in a soft, low voice, in a rhythm so calm I felt comforted. In one hand she held the wing of a large bird and fanned it slowly over me.

The sun was high when I awoke. William sat on the floor at my side, spinning his top between his legs. He leaned over to get a good look at my face, then placed a new pair of moccasins by my chin. The beadwork was in rows of green, white, and blue. They were beautiful.

"For you, Carrie," he said. "Nig and Stumpy ate your boots."

I stroked his yellow hair, then touched my wound. It was healed.

The next few weeks passed quickly. Every day Dick and Junior were gone until sundown, hunting and checking their beaver traps upriver. Jenny always looked at me gently, so it was hard for me to act mad and even harder to think of running away.

The nicer she was, though, the more I missed my own mother.

After breakfast one morning, I took the griddle to the river and scrubbed it with gravel. A twig cracked behind me. When I saw what had made the noise, I tried to scream but no sound came.

5

"the indans that was out hunting the teton range as got a big scair an thay say thare is war parteys of the suex [Sioux] indans in the range"

25 August 1875

Four Indians on horseback stared at me from a few feet away. One had hair hanging to his shoulders; the others had long braids tied at the ends with buckskin. Each held a rifle in his arms. Their faces were like stone.

My feet wouldn't move. Suddenly my terror turned to anger and I raised the skillet, backing slowly into the river, a hiss in my breath. Out of the corner of my eye, I could see the cabin where the children played. Jenny worked in the sun over a hide. Somebody, please!

Then John saw me and started running. "Mother!" he shouted. "Two Eagle is back. Hello!"

32

The Indians now reined their horses toward John, although the one with the feather by his ear kept looking back at me. A slight smile formed on his lips, but I kept the pan high.

Two Eagle slid from his horse and walked up to Jenny. He pointed to the far mountains that stood white beyond the valley. As he spoke, he drew his hands first near his face, then in front of his chest. I couldn't understand Shoshoni or his signs, but Jenny did.

She turned toward the cabin and disappeared inside. When she came out, she was carrying a six-shooter under one arm and a breech-loading rifle under the other. It looked just like my father's Betsy. She set them in the dirt at our feet and stood next to John.

"Sioux warriors are in the Tetons," John said to me. "Maybe three suns away. Two Eagle and his brothers will ride word to Fort Hall." His shoulders were as straight and brave as a seven-year-old's could be. With Dick and Junior gone, he was now man of the house, as my brother Samuel had loved to be. "Do not worry, Carrie," John said.

The four Indians rode into the aspens, disappearing as silently as they had come.

For the past few days, Jenny had been showing me how to dry chokecherries and serviceberries on a hide in the sun.

"They are good to eat in the winter," she had said. "You will like the pudding I make from them." She was also going to sew some into a rawhide ball for Elisabeth to rattle.

Jenny held a basket between her knees as Anne Jane smoked a fire next to us to keep yellow jackets off the fruit. William and John started stacking stones in play. Elisabeth slept in her cradleboard under a pine.

Without looking up, Jenny began to talk about a war party from long ago. "I was fourteen winters when Henri LaFleure came to camp with beaver pelts on his mules. My father, Fast Horse, and the other men were quiet as they played the hand game near our night fire. Henri LaFleure stood when he won. He looked at my mother, Singing Grass, and bowed his head."

Jenny's hands were stained purple. The juice squeezed from the berries had almost filled a small wooden bowl. She kept her eyes down.

"Our marriage was the next day. The custom of Chief Washakie's people was to enjoy a long courtship, while the bride's aunts and sisters helped sew her lodge. But the first snows were near and Henri LaFleure had much trading left. He was now my husband, and I would be going with him after the next sun.

"On our wedding night, he lay a buffalo robe in the willows away from the others. In the darkness, he talked to me, you know. I could not understand the words, but I did understand he wanted me to love him. *J'aime Henri* was what he had me say again and again.

"While he slept, I watched the Star People. It was very dark when I heard something. It was in the camp, and it was not good," she said.

Two squirrels watched us from a rock, their tails ruffling in the breeze. It seemed they were listening, too. Jenny's hands stopped, and she studied a cloud passing in front of the sun.

"A child cried," she continued. "Then its mother screamed. So much screaming. I crawled quickly into the trees with the bundle of my dress in my mouth. A log lay over a stream. It made a low bridge in the cold water. I hid under it until the screams stopped, until the sun moved into darkness, and until another sun came. The smell of smoke and flesh burning saved my stomach from hunger. My ear was against the pebbles. My braids floated in front of my face. I stretched my mouth into the water to drink.

"This way I listened. A sound inside the stones told me horses were coming near. I did not move.

"Soon a voice stopped the quiet. I saw two mares and a mule, then the moccasins of a *tybo*—a white man—in a saddle. His leggings were fringed like Henri LaFleure's. I pulled myself from under the log, slowly, as I was stiff with cold. When he saw me he reached for his gun but stopped."

Jenny stood and walked to the tree where Elisabeth was. She carried the cradleboard back to where we sat and propped it against a rock. Now Elisabeth watched us with her quiet brown eyes. Jenny formed several patties from the berries and laid them on the hide before continuing.

"I saw at last what happened to my people during the night of my wedding. What I saw of Henri LaFleure made my hand cover my mouth. But it was the sight of my mother that made me fall to the ground.

"*Nabia-tsee.* My dear mother. She was on her back with her dress pulled above her breasts.

Blood was on her thighs. The wound on her head moved with flies.

"The lodge where I had lived only two sleeps ago was still standing.

"Its flap was torn open so I could see my father and my youngest sister, Blue Egg."

This was the first time Jenny had talked so much to me. Her English was even better than Beaver Dick's. I wanted to ask her questions, but I stayed silent. Her story filled me with rage. Maybe someday I would be able to tell her what her people did to my family.

"Blackfeet," she said, looking at me as if she'd heard my thoughts. "I knew their sign, moccasins turned in at the toes. Crow might do such a thing, but this war party was Blackfeet. They were after our horses. I did not know why they would want to kill, too.

"The white man dug many graves. I smoothed the dirt over the mound of my parents and sisters, then laid a branch of pine on top. With a flint I stabbed at my arms and legs. I cut my hair as my mother had done when her sister died in childbed.

"The *tybo,* he spoke like Henri LaFleure. He was very kind the way he looked at me. I tried to understand him. I said the only white-man words I knew, *J'aime Henri,* over and over, until he tried to say them, too."

Jenny's shoulders began to move in her slow way of laughing. Her teeth were white and even. Anne Jane kneeled next to her mother, eager to laugh, too.

"He thought I said 'Jenny.' Then he made a sign like this." She tapped two fingers on her chest.

"He said his name. But to me he is Ingabumbee: 'red hair.'"

Elisabeth cooed. Jenny unlaced the leather and nursed her through a flap in her dress. Anne Jane tipped the bowl of juice to drink, then passed it to William, who had made a miniature fort from stones. John watched us from the other side of the river.

"Now I am called Jenny," she said. "My name from my family is buried with them."

6

*"it frose ice last night the teton mountins are as white with
snow as if it was winter time"*

28 August 1875

A creak of the door woke me. The fire had gone
out, and the room was gray with dawn. Footsteps
outside my window set my heart to pounding.

Slowly I raised myself up so my nose touched
the rough wood of the sill, my eyeballs wide at the
glass. My breath came fast.

An Indian wrapped in a buffalo robe walked
away from the cabin. I could see only the black hair
and the steady puffs of frost in front of his face. At
the river he stopped, untied his moccasins, and let
the robe fall to the bank. His hair hung loose down
his back. He was naked.

Just then a peek of sun rose from the east, and

he turned to face the first rays. Instantly, I realized *he* was a *she*!

I looked quickly at Jenny's pallet in the corner, but it was empty. Dick was gone, too. By the time I looked back, she was in the water, one hand holding her hair above her head, the other splashing her face and under her arms.

I burrowed into the woolly hair of my robe. The bucket of water by the hearth was frozen solid. Why anybody would want to jump in a river with no clothes on when it was colder than Christmas didn't make a peanut of sense to me.

Like most civilized folks, Mother had always heated a kettle. If Father had seen her naked in ice water he would have hauled her into the house to worry over her.

Poor Mother.

There it was again: that hot feeling inside. I had to push it away so it wouldn't boil up into a scream. Mother! Lately I'd been pinching my knee, trying to make *it* hurt instead of my heart. Jenny might be in my mother's place but she would never replace her.

I watched out the window. Jenny sat wrapped in her robe, her face to the sun. Her mouth moved slightly as if in song, and I strained to listen. The river washed and roared over the boulders. Her voice reached me on the breeze, just as sunlight from the other window spread against my cheek.

Last night's frost had killed the garden. Jenny bent over the neat rows as Dick rode into sight. He was back early, which I'd learned meant one of two things, danger or adventure—a thought that pained me on this cold morning.

"All we 'ave now is a mess of peas, looks like," he said. He rolled a ball of lettuce along the ground, scattering a family of chipmunks who'd been preening in the sun. A buck was draped over Dick's packhorse, steam rising off the still-warm body. Its antlers had twelve points and later would be hung above the door, racked with guns.

"Peas 'n' piss," he said. He unfolded a note from his pocket. "There's big trouble up to Lyons's place, poor old man. 'Is sons beat 'im silly with a club, and now they're tryin' t'steal 'is money. This message was nailed to the tree by 'is well."

Elisabeth had waddled into the garden. Junior's derby hid her head, but she was otherwise bare as a birch. William slipped his hand into mine.

"Saddle up, Junior. We're off to see justice done," Dick said. As he spoke, he threw a rope over the branch of a white pine and hoisted the buck by its hind legs, high enough to be clear of a dog's leap.

"Jenny and Carrie, Mrs. Lyons needs your 'ands of comfort. The sons broke their old man's 'ead but they broke their mother's 'eart."

It took only a few minutes before we were ready to leave. Everyone moved into action so fast I felt like a gatepost.

Jenny appeared with several tall branches that had been stripped clean and tied together at both ends with rawhide. She placed them and some bundles of hide onto a sled hitched to the sides of her horse by long poles. She called this sled a travois.

William dressed Elisabeth in a long shirt, then settled the two of them among the hides. While I thought of packing my mirror and other vanities, Dick led a spotted yearling to me.

"'Bout time you folks met, Missie." The horse had a red blanket in place of a saddle, and since there were no stirrups, Dick boosted me aboard. There was nothing to hang on to! I nearly slipped off.

"I shook my brain for a name for 'er and come up with Carry-Me-'Ome." Dick laced my hands into the mane. It was long and warm in my fingers.

I tried a smile.

"That way, you'll always come 'ome to us, Missie." He slapped her rump and we were off.

I hung on for dear life. We were like a train pulling out of town, slow and bumpy. Dick led. John and Anne Jane followed on their horses; then came Jenny on her mare, Bony. William and Elisabeth giggled from the travois as it dragged along the ground behind Bony.

Junior was the caboose. Carry-Me-Home seemed to know she had a greenhorn on her back, because she didn't try anything fancy. Eventually my fingers loosened, and I sat up straight. By the time we nooned, the blanket felt as easy as the moccasins on my feet. The insides of my legs weren't raw like they'd been on the trip from Fort Hall.

"Lyons's place is another hour's ride north, so we'll camp here," Dick said as he loaded his rifle. Jenny was standing under a triangle of poles that were lashed together near the top. While I wondered how I could help, she leaned more poles against the others—nine in all—wrapping their tips with the rope that dangled from the top. In and out she weaved, her arms up and her dress billowing in the wind, round and round. My eyes filled with tears.

I remembered my own mother showing me the Maypole dance, happy that she'd safely delivered a new son and happy that our wagons were loaded for Oregon. I remembered the way Father watched her dance and the way he kissed her afterward.

Suddenly I hated Jenny. I didn't want to love her. There wasn't enough room. As I tried to think awful things about her, Anne Jane unfolded a huge canvas and Jenny wrapped it around the frame, leaving an opening at the top. The sticks poked up like winter branches. She opened a low flap, then ducked in. John handed her the sleeping robes, and Junior hammered stakes until the tent stretched tight toward the ground.

Elisabeth backed herself into my lap. My arms immediately circled her, and I rubbed my face in her warm hair.

Our quiet was interrupted by the blast of a gun and a man's shout.

7

*"alven struck his father 8 times in the face and John
[Lyons] snatched a duble barl rifall when i turned
my gun on him and made him lay it downe he sead
he was going to shoot me"*

Summer 1875

"*Dammit to 'ell,* you stupid roan!"

We ran toward the creek where Beaver Dick lay
sprawled in the mud. His horse was bucking, a
wild sage hen flapping her wings underfoot.

It seemed funny to see Dick mad as a wet cat,
but I didn't laugh when I saw what he did next.

He reached for his rifle, which had fallen in a
bush, and swung it at the horse's head. Crack, it
landed by the ears.

"Damn beast!" he yelled, swinging again.

He cracked the gun on its nose. Its eyes were
wide and scared as it tried to pull away.

"Stop it, stop it!" Now the yell was mine. I ran between them, wrapped my arms around the horse's neck, and screwed my eyes shut. I didn't care if he whacked me, too.

"Dammit, girl, what the fool bells y'doin'?"

"You're hurting her," I said, my hands still locked in the mane. "She didn't throw you on purpose."

His hair dripped in his face, hair redder than ever with the sun now behind him. I didn't know grown-ups had temper tantrums; and what's more, I didn't know if I liked this mountain man anymore.

"Now it's bent, kee-riste almighty." He squinted through the sight. The barrel looked like a crooked finger. He began pounding it against a rock, but before he could straighten it, shots rang in the distance—first one, then another.

Dick jumped into his saddle. "Wait 'ere with the little ones," he hollered over his shoulder to Jenny. "Junior, move it!" Then he looked back at me.

"You stay put, Missie."

Maybe it was the bossy way he said it, or maybe it was because I was mad at him, but as soon as he and Junior disappeared through the trees, I raced to Carry-Me-Home.

"We'll show that smelly ol' barbarian," I whispered on her cheek. The first leap, I slid over her back to the other side. Two more jumps and I was only hanging from her neck. Then I felt a hand under my foot, and with a gentle boost, I was up.

"Careful, Ohabumbee," Jenny said. She was helping for some reason, and for a second I wanted to like her.

Then Carry-Me-Home lurched forward and off we went. I didn't know what I was doing or how to stay on at a gallop, but somehow I managed to keep my legs squeezed against her sides and my fingers knotted in her mane. Through the trees, into a clearing, and to the edge of a canyon, we followed Beaver Dick.

The Lyons's cabin stood in a grove of aspens. Smoke curled up from the chimney, and the scene was peaceful except for the shouting. Dick's and Junior's horses grazed by the creek.

"Stay, baby." I kissed the velvet end of her nose. "You'll be safe here."

Why I imagined I could take on the Lyons boys, I'll never know. They had guns, and all I had right now was a bunch of nothing. My anger and my hurt had stirred a recklessness inside that I hadn't known was there.

"You're a murderer, Beaver Dick," a voice yelled from the cabin. "A lyin' sonofabitch." I crept closer so I could see through the window.

Dick had aimed his crooked gun at a large fellow who was choking an old man around the neck.

"You've met your match, Alvin," Dick said. "Let 'im go, or I'll turn y'into dog food. Now!"

Alvin loosened his hands enough for Mr. Lyons to scramble to the four-poster where his wife sat weeping. They hugged each other.

"Put it away, John," another man said. The voice sounded familiar, but it wasn't Junior's. I crept closer. In front of the hearth, John Lyons had someone pinned facedown on the stones, a club of firewood against the man's back.

"You don't want to hurt anyone, John Boy, so put it down," the voice said again from the floor. Then he eased his head around and I saw his profile.

Miles Alexander! How'd he get here?

There was a path of rocks at my feet. Slowly I

reached down and dug with my fingers until one fit in my hand. I took a deep breath. "Drop it or die, cow face!" Then, not knowing what else to say, I copied Dick. "If I have to use this, you'll be dog food. Now!"

John Lyons turned toward me but by the time he saw it was only a girl, Miles had twisted free. He kicked John off his feet and in the same instant wrestled the club into his own hands.

"Well," Miles said as he bound John's arms with a belt. "I would've shaved if I knew you were coming for supper, Carrie."

Beaver Dick still seemed mad, but I did catch a half smile when he looked my way.

"Alvin Lyons and John Lyons, you are under arrest," Dick said. "We'll see what the sheriff in Malad City 'as to say about you snakes. Cattle rustlin' and money grubbin' is jail time, boys."

Then he grabbed the front of Alvin's shirt and twisted it so tight the man's face turned dark. "And for 'urtin' your folks," he hissed, "you should be 'ung from the tallest tree till your boots pop."

A short time after, two other trapper friends of Dick's rode up. They had been skinning elk downstream when they heard the shots. Mountain men felt duty-bound to step in at any sign of trouble.

"Tom Lavering, John Hogue, we need your 'elp getting these thieves to justice," he told them after making introductions. Then Dick handed Mr. Lyons a roll of dollar bills thick enough to choke a horse. "Believe this belongs t'you, sir."

Miles smiled at me every time I looked over at him, which I tried not to do. He was too handsome for my heart right now.

While the Lyons boys were roped safely on the floor, I tended to their parents. Poor folks, so scared and shaky.

"I once ran for mayor of New York City," Mr. Lyons told me. "But the wife and I, we wanted a few quiet days before we go..." He rubbed his forehead. "Who would've thought that at seventy-two years of age I'd have to beg protection from our own sons? God bless Beaver Dick is all I can say."

We left the old couple before dusk. Dick had shot an antelope and, with Junior's help, dressed it so the Lyonses would have fresh meat. Tom Lavering and Mr. Hogue axed a new stack of wood, while the prisoners waited on horseback, tied to the saddles.

Carry-Me-Home must not have understood her new name, because she was nowhere in sight. Junior said not to worry; she was more'n likely back at camp nuzzling up to Bony.

It was not an unpleasant coincidence that Miles had a space in his saddle for a girl about my size. I tried to ignore his chest against my back as we moved south. I kept my hands on the horn and by the time we spotted Jenny's tipi through the trees, it was almost dark. We hadn't said one word to each other since Miles's apology for not shaving.

When he lifted me from the saddle, I felt his breath by my ear. His hands held my waist a moment longer than they needed to.

Jenny's kettle simmered with stew. After supper, Dick caught Alvin unhobbling the horses to make a getaway, so from then on the Lyons boys lay tied up near the fire with three rifles pointed their way.

The stars were bright overhead when Jenny ushered the children into the lodge. I folded Elisabeth into my robe. Through the canvas I watched the shadows of the men against the firelight.

Their voices were low, but I could hear their teasing.

"Rides all the way up Lyons Crik to be an angel of mercy, but by God if his gun ain't wrinkled as my big toe."

Laughter. Someone poked the fire with his boot, sending a spray of sparks skyward. My eyes felt heavy.

"Then we got the carpenter here, held up by a piece of wood. Damned if that ain't a skunk in the milk house."

"Well, as I say, gentlemen,"—the voice was Miles's—"surprises are what keep the days bright."

More laughter. I tried to listen, but the next thing I knew it was morning, and they were gone.

8

"the yellow Jackitts are in swarms by hundreds for 15 mills [miles] the length of the timber on the north fork me and tom gets stung very ofton wile handling fresh meat or fish"

6 September 1875

The air was cool. The cottonwoods and aspen had turned bright yellow and gold. Mountain bluebirds were flying south in wide Vs, soaring under gray clouds. Jenny watched the sky.

"Snows are near," she said.

By sundown, two tipis were pitched near the cabin by Shoshoni on their way south from their fall hunt.

It still made me nervous to see many Indians, so I watched from the safety of my window. Jenny took them baskets of dried berries and jerky while Junior watered their horses. A drum beat as voices sang in a wail so high it sent a shiver down my spine.

Jenny returned to nurse Elisabeth. It was dark except for the bonfires outside.

"Do not worry, Carrie." She must have felt my thoughts. "No one will hurt you."

I almost rushed to lay my head in her lap but held back. Elisabeth sucked loudly at her breast. John, Anne Jane, and William slept under their furs.

"Is that a war song?" I looked at her profile in the light that flickered across the room. Her cheekbones were high in a face I could only think of as beautiful. I watched her looking out and felt sorry I'd been mad at her.

"Their son was murdered by white men twelve sleeps ago."

I wasn't sure I wanted to hear the story.

"They were hunting on the other side of the Tetons," she said, still staring out. "They were near a *tybo* ranch on Jackson Lake. Humpy stole a horse, so the white men shot him, but he did not die. They tied him with rocks to see if that Indian could float."

Jenny tucked Elisabeth under the robe on her

pallet. The drum outside pounded on. "Humpy's family grieves because he sleeps at the bottom of a lake. His spirit will be far away from home."

Well, serves him right, I wanted to say. Stealing is wrong no matter how you look at it. But as we sat in the darkness, I remembered Alvin and John Lyons. Beaver Dick said they were well known in these parts as rustlers and no-goods. Right now those white boys were eating cobbler in a jail cell, probably telling each other jokes. For their thieving, they got a day in court. Humpy got a bullet.

I was beginning to understand how Father felt.

The tipis stayed several days. Grandmother Humpy came to me when I was at the river rinsing my petticoats. She spoke softly, with a smile that lifted her whole face. She pointed toward Jenny, then crossed her arms, and then opened her palm by my face.

I couldn't understand her signs, but I got the idea she wanted me to feel safe. A pigtailed girl about Elisabeth's age appeared from behind a willow, then quickly hid herself in the old woman's blanket. She peeked out to hand me a doll. It fit in my palm: a miniature Indian in a buckskin dress adorned with beadwork. She wanted me to keep it.

"Thank you." I bent to touch her, but she ducked behind her grandmother.

"Thank you, Shy One." They walked back to their camp. A hint of happiness fluttered inside me.

As soon as the sun dropped, the air froze. Tom Lavering and Mr. Hogue came in for the evening. Jenny roasted a side of ribs and fried two skillets of johnnycake.

"Dick, you got yourself three boys," Tom said with his mouth full. He lifted his beard and wiped his lips with it.

"Tell me something new, Lavering."

"Wonderin', why'n't we take 'em tomorrow upriver t'check the mink traps?"

"Well, sir, that ain't a bad idea," Dick answered, "but I learned me a lesson a while back."

He pulled a few ribs from the spit and handed them to Jenny in his bowl. He winked at her.

"One boy is a job done. Two boys is a job 'alf done. But three boys,"—he laughed—"now, that ain't a lick of work done atall."

"Well, well."

"They frisk about like tomorrow ain't coming till next year. 'Sides, them winged varmints will eat the little ones alive."

John, William, and Junior exchanged grins, obviously pleased that they were the topic of conversation. William took the opportunity to pull Anne Jane's hair and slug her arm. With barely a flip, she pinned him to the ground and sat on him. Then John tried to knock her over just as Elisabeth dove for the pile. Shrieks and screams for help blasted the calm.

"Enough!" Dick pulled the children apart and plopped them in separate corners. Junior leaned against the hearth with the superiority of an eleven-year-old who knows he has narrowly missed punishment.

Jenny opened a small trunk and unwrapped a bundle of cloth. Inside was a fiddle. She handed it to Dick.

"Play for us, Ingabumbee."

"Yes, Oppah, play," Junior said.

"Please," the others begged.

And how he did. Tom reached into his vest and soon was playing along with his mouth harp.

Mr. Hogue slapped his knees in time. "Dance Little Joe," "My Sweetheart Loves Me True," and several other tunes set my toes to jig.

When the fire was just coals, Tom and Mr. Hogue spread out their bedrolls, and the rest of us slid between our own robes. I was almost asleep when I noticed Dick leaning toward the fireplace, a notebook in his lap. He was writing!

I thought mountain men only shot deer and wore greasy hats. As his pencil moved carefully across the page, it reminded me that I hadn't written in my journal since early July, when our wagon train was camped by the Sublette cutoff. Mother had baked a sugar cake because it was Joey's fifth birthday. And that night, Father had helped a Mrs. Henry bring forth twin daughters.

9

*"i made a dineing table for my famly this is the first
real table we ever ad in the mountins."*

1 October 1875

By the end of September everything in sight was dusted with snow. Dick had nailed a thermometer to the eaves by my window, and this morning it read twelve degrees.

Though Jenny had coaxed the coals into a blaze, the room was cold. There were dots of white on the walls from ice-covered nails. My breathing made puffs of frost. A run to the outhouse would be misery, so I stretched back into the fur and thought about using the bucket in the corner.

"Jenny!" Beaver Dick yelled from outside. "We got two new neighbors come t'welcome themselves with breakfast."

She continued to work over the fire. The large coffeepot sat on the edge of the coals, rattling with steam. She dropped in two handfuls of grounds.

"And they brung a fat ol' elk for the spit. Come in, boys."

The door crashed open. Dick marched to the fire with an armful of bloody steaks. He wore knee-high moccasins of fur that left snowy footprints on the floor. Jenny skewered the meat and set it to roast.

Next came Tom Lavering, big in a coat of pelts and with a howdy for us. The children moved under their robes like sleepy cubs. I fumbled for my clothes and found that my blanket had frozen to the wall.

Then in came Tom's friend, also big and furry. When he saw me, he shook the snow out of his hair and bowed to me.

Miles Alexander had a knack for showing up at the oddest moments.

"A radiant beauty brings light to our day," he said, waving his hand to his ankle. There was a merry look to his eyes.

"Oh, it's you." I sank into my robe while my

foot searched frantically for my dress. It had disappeared.

While the smell of cooking meat filled the room, they drank coffee and jawed about the cabin Miles and Tom had just finished upstream. They were now trapping partners with Beaver Dick. This breakfast could take all day, and I was not about to squat on a chamber pot in front of everyone.

I wrapped myself in the old buffalo skin, stood, and—without looking at any of the faces turned my way—stumbled toward the door. The robe dragged at least one cup of coffee to its side.

One bare foot into the snow, I realized this was no grassy stroll in Missouri. It was, however, the fastest sprint this girl ever made. A colder seat was never so welcome.

Just when I was ready for the return run, the door opened. Jenny closed herself inside. She held a pile of clothes.

"You will be warm in these," she said. Her braids were wrapped in otter skins. As she stood next to me, I realized I wasn't afraid to look at her face anymore. For the first time, I noticed her eyes: brown, of course. But what kept me staring was the thin ring of blue that encircled the brown, as perfectly as sky encircles the earth.

"Your eyes," I started. Maybe she had never seen herself in a mirror. Maybe she didn't know there was something unusual about her. She returned to the path. *You're special,* I thought.

The leggings were of soft deerskin, as was the dress that hung below my knees. New moccasins tied above my ankles. The fur inside was warm. I combed my fingers through my hair and fashioned two braids. Even with old Mr. Buffalo over my shoulders, I knew I was the loveliest white girl in these mountains. When Miles saw me, he would faint with admiration. I readied myself for praise.

Jenny turned from the fire when I walked in. The children were also dressed in skins and didn't seem surprised that we looked alike. The men were gone.

"Junior went to get a surprise for Mother," John said. He chewed a chunk of meat from his knife.

"They'll be back for supper with a big surprise," William said, landing a jump on Anne Jane's foot. She whacked him, then pushed him to the floor.

It was going to be a long day.

Late afternoon saw a small procession moving our way. The cart behind Junior's mare had something bulky hidden under a canvas. A colt pranced beside its mother. Two milk cows followed, bells clanging from their necks, and Nig and Stumpy at their heels. Beaver Dick rode ahead with the news.

"Your son done some trading, Jenny; something you never seen the likes of. And the carpenter helped me fancy up a table." The smile through his mangy beard even made me grin. "Tonight we dine!"

The thing under the canvas was a cookstove, a big iron thing with a well for burning wood and an oven. Junior bought it from Mr. Kaiser for his black filly, one silver dollar, and a badger he had speared with a hayfork.

If Miles noticed my new outfit, he didn't let on. He and Tom were busy dressing two deer, careful to save the full hides for Jenny. I fluttered around the cabin like a parlor maid before the banquet.

There still were no chairs, so we ate around Dick's table from an assortment of wobbly boxes and upended logs. Our mouths were so full that hardly a word was spoken. Boiled yamps tasted as sweet as buttered carrots, and the goose was roasted so tender you could swallow after one chew. Antelope steaks and mint pudding. Jenny baked a flatbread oozing with blackberry jam. It was the most delicious meal I'd had in a long time.

Which set me to remembering. If I squinted, these folks could be my own. Father laughing. Mother up and down to the stove. The children giggling and shoving each other. Company laughing, too. Suddenly I couldn't listen anymore. I was not about to start weeping in front of a bunch of strangers.

It was frosty out. I waited by the river until its roar made everything else seem quiet. Ice formed in small crescents near the shore. Someone stood behind me.

Jenny.

Without thinking, without caring how she felt, I blubbered out the feelings that had been fermenting inside.

"I hate what your people did to my family."

For several moments she watched the sky. "We have each lost a family," she said. Her voice was calm. "Now we share one."

"It's not the same."

Jenny stepped forward, then turned to face me. "If we care for those we are with, we will not miss the others so much."

Hooey.

"You and William are *ohabumbee*: 'yellow hair.' To my children, you are a sister."

"I'm an orphan and I'll never forget it."

"There are no orphans among Indian people."

You don't know what it's like, I almost screamed. But she did know. Jenny and I had a bond I was slow to admit.

It happened so fast that hot July day. Thunder shook the earth from black clouds overhead. There was so much noise, at first I didn't hear Father's shout.

Painted riders on horses raced in a circle around our wagons. Guns fired. Mother pushed me down by the wheels, but she fell. Ivan was in her arms. I felt a sting on my forehead so I lay still. Soon it was over.

What I saw filled me with anguish. Riders were galloping off, each holding a small bundle in front of them. I realized as they rode away that the cries fading with them in the distance were those of children. White children.

———

"I am sorry for your pain, Carrie." She looked down the valley, where the river snaked its way south. The evening star grew bright in the darkening sky.

"*Tybo* bring too many white buffalo. Our fields are crushed. They force my people away from their home." She pulled her blanket up to her chin.

If there hadn't been such a stubborn goat in me, I would have hugged her with all my might. Instead, we just looked at each other. Our breaths met midair. I blinked my eyes to keep from crying and slowly managed a smile for Jenny. It was the first.

10

"some indans came hear they ad shot a Boflo [buffalo]
Bull Braking his hind leg... this is the first Buflo that
as beene seene since the spring of 1871."

2 October 1875

After breakfast the next morning, Dick un-
hooked the Betsy from the wall and handed it to
me. It was heavy. The wood was long and smooth.

"Time you learned t'shoot, Missie." He hefted
his saddle onto his shoulder and walked toward
the corral. "Junior is 'elping Mr. Kaiser chase two
'undred 'ead of cattle into Montana. I'm escorting
'im up the north fork."

Miles sat in the sun by the woodpile, a cup of
coffee on his knee. His hair curled above his collar,
and—as he was the only man in these woods without a beard—his jaw was a handsome sight. The

67

quiet way he looked at me put a butterfly inside. With Miles for a teacher, I could learn to shoot a fly on the moon.

"Missie," Dick yelled as he and Junior rode out. He pointed to the river where Jenny waited with her rifle.

I looked back at Miles. He grinned.

"She's a better shot than I am, Carrie," he said, "and if you want to know the eagle's truth, she can outshoot Ingabumbee any day. But don't tell him I told y'so." He slapped his leg with his hat and set his cup on a stump. "I'll see you gals later."

"You late for a quilting bee?" Now I was mad. Miles had a habit of appearing when I didn't want him to and *disappearing* when I didn't want him to. "There's a pile of dishes in there, you know."

He laughed. When he stood next to me, I only came up to his chest pocket. He squeezed my arm gently, then started loading his rifle.

"Mr. Davis lost one of his cows to a grizzly the other night. He stuffed his bear trap with three dead beavers, fat ones." Miles slipped a six-shooter into a fold of his saddle and cinched the stirrup.

"Old Griz sprung the trap, ate those beavers fur and all, then ran off. He's still around, 'cause Davis found fresh tracks by his barn."

Be careful, I wanted to say. But, instead, I pretended to yawn and headed for Jenny. He was laughing when he took off.

John stretched scraps of flannel on thornbushes across the river. He drew target circles on them with charcoal then sat downstream to watch.

Jenny hit a bull's-eye seven shots out of nine. On the tenth, she lowered her gun.

"You try, Ohabumbee."

The children giggled, ready for a show. I didn't let them down. It was high noon before Betsy and I even hit a target. I managed to blast every bush in sight. After lunch, my shoulder was so sore from the gun's kickback, I quit.

Jenny pulled Elisabeth into her lap as we leaned against the sunny side of the cabin. Anne Jane laid her head on her mother's arm. Their dark hair blended together, and their dresses of deerskin looked so soft I wanted to lie with them. I wanted to be a daughter again.

Jenny saw me watching. It was getting easier for me to smile at her and it felt good.

"Come, Ohabumbee." She opened her other arm for me.

Miles and Tom arrived just before sundown.

"No griz," Miles said. He ate opposite Jenny while I minded the stove.

"What would you do if you found him?" I asked, bending over him with a ladle of stew.

"Why, kill him, of course."

"How?"

He turned to look at me. His mouth was full. After he swallowed he narrowed his eyes.

"Bullet. Clean through the heart if the Good Maker's watching me."

"Just because he ate a cow?"

"Put it to you this way, Carrie." He exchanged a disbelieving look with Tom. "If Old Griz can eat a cow, he sure as heck can eat you, and eat you he will if he and I don't meet eye to eye."

"Well, maybe he's gone to sleep for the winter now."

He laughed. "With a cow and those beavers in

his belly, I'd venture a guess you're right. Should last him till spring."

"Then, come spring, him and Miles can polka." Tom laughed so hard crumbs spewed out of his mouth. The children promptly imitated him with their own mouthfuls of bread, which perked the dogs' interest. Nig and Stumpy circled the table, barking and wagging their tails.

Jenny slapped her fingers on the edge of the table. The uproar stopped and the dogs slipped back to their posts by the door.

"The white bear gives us much," she said. "We must eat and we must be warm. We must also protect ourselves. The animal understands this. This way is fair."

More and more I wondered about fair. Father knew its meaning. I wished he were here to explain things.

"When I was ten winters, you know, these valleys moved with buffalo." Her eyes were down. "There are *tybo* who kill for fun. I have seen their waste. The animals don't understand this. I don't understand this."

Miles stroked my braid. "That's why Ingabumbee

wants you and Betsy to be good friends, Carrie," he said. "If you can protect yourself, more'n likely you'll never go hungry. Take what you need, leave the rest to roam, and it'll be there to help you out the next time."

I couldn't tell from Jenny's face what she was thinking, but as she stood she placed her hand on Miles's. He winked at me.

11

*"the cuntry is all on fire from the south fork canon
to the midle fork . . . most of the snake river cuntry as
beene burnt . . . 5 lodges [tipis] of indans camped near
my cabin thay braught me word from my son
richard he is at henrys lake."*

4–5 October 1875

$\mathcal{S}$*moke from the north* rose in large puffs, then
stopped.

"Bannocks," Jenny said. Dick stood next to her.

"They found buffalo." He looked to the west
where another column of smoke rose in smaller
clouds. "'Unters will come."

This was the strangest message I'd ever seen.
How they knew who was saying what was a mys-
tery I'd probably never understand.

We were about two miles upriver, dressing
Dick's trappings while he took the boat after more.
At the water's edge, Jenny worked over the hide of
a large buck shot that morning. Anne Jane and I

73

had dug the ticks out of its fur and now Jenny scraped its underside. Her hands were wet with blood. The ground was dry again, since most of the snow had melted.

Elisabeth copied us with a rabbit skin that John gave her. For a long while she rolled a stick over it, back and forth; then she started to rub her eyes.

"Goh-no," she said, pointing to her cradleboard.

Jenny looked up and shook her head. "You are a big girl now, *tsee-tsee*. Where will your doll sleep?" She smiled.

"Goh-no," Elisabeth said again. Her lower lip turned down into a cry. Jenny nodded to me.

"Here you go, sweetheart." I picked her up with an *oomph* and held her against the board while I laced her in, arms crossed over her chest. She barely fit anymore. Immediately she closed her eyes and was asleep. It felt like I was lifting a log when I carried her to a sunny spot in the grass.

"You were the same, daughter," Jenny said to Anne Jane, who was laughing. "You tried to take little John out of his." This report pleased Anne Jane, and I laughed, too.

We worked on while William and John skipped pebbles into the water. Jays hopped in the brush nearby, squawking for a free meal. The sun soaked through my clothes and warmed me. The fragrance of pine filled the air. If someone had held me tight, I would have fallen asleep as peacefully as Elisabeth had.

A scream pierced the quiet. John was running toward us. "Mother, hurry!" He pointed to the sky. Black smoke billowed our way.

Jenny stood. Her face showed no change, but she immediately pulled Anne Jane into the stream.

I reached William, and with a leap we were both in the middle of the icy current. I held his head up and kicked with my legs to keep us afloat. My dress wrapped around my legs until I thought it would pull me under. My feet felt for the bottom. John was splashing with Anne Jane. Now I could see the fire.

It pushed through the trees along the shore, feeding on the yellow grass. Sparks shot into the water.

Then I saw Elisabeth. Sound asleep right where I'd left her, flames moving steadily her way. Jenny was waist deep, pulling with her arms for the bank. She would never make it in time.

Just then she fell onto the bloodied hide and grabbed an edge. With a lunge she heaved it toward Elisabeth. The hide landed on the cradleboard, covering it completely. Jenny dove back into the water.

My foot slipped along a boulder until I could brace myself, a shivering William in my arms. Anne Jane and John had reached the far shore. Jenny hung on to a branch wedged in the rocks. We all watched in horror as the fire passed over Elisabeth.

"Our baby!" Anne Jane wailed.

Then thick smoke covered us. We coughed and choked until I thought we might all die. The fire hurried south. In a few moments it was gone, a smoldering trail of black in its wake.

Jenny was already on shore, stumbling toward the singed hump. When she peeled the hide away, she fell to her knees. Elisabeth was bawling loudly. She was alive.

William and I were shaking from the cold and my legs were numb by the time we dragged ourselves to shore. The horses had scattered downriver. Nothing was left from our packs except chunks of melted silver.

Halfway home we heard shouts through the trees.

Miles kicked into full speed when he saw us. Several Indians rode single-file behind him.

Then there were warm robes around us. Beaver Dick held Jenny's face in his hands before wrapping Elisabeth in his cape.

As we walked, feeling came back to my feet. Miles stayed at my side. The aroma of roasting meat greeted us; then we saw Grandmother Humpy and Shy One. Five tipis formed a half circle by the cabin, and in the center crackled a welcome fire.

It was good to be home.

12

"all the buty and Grandur of the tetons and the range of mountins can be seene to the best adventge and the teton bason itselfe is one of the butifullist mountin vallys and camp grounds to be seene in the rocky mountins"

Letter to the editor, date unknown

Winter.

The days were short and cold, the nights colder. Dick's windup clock ticked the dark hours away. Firelight and oil lamps were our warm companions.

One morning I woke to something wet on my cheek. A snowflake. We spent the day boiling mud in a kettle and smearing it with twigs into cracks between the logs. After that, the wind reached us only from under the door.

Dick and Junior tracked on snowshoes. When they returned empty-handed, Jenny fed us well with her stock of dried meat. There was always plenty of gravy, potatoes, and berries.

One raw afternoon before Christmas, a visitor called. The sound of sleigh bells reached us across the frozen valley before she did. A large woman in a velvet cape and high laced boots stepped down from the runners like Queen Victoria at the opera. Her bonnet framed a round face that looked accustomed to laughing. Her cheeks and nose were red with cold.

"Alice Mitten, folks," she said, surveying our cabin. "I'm a widow lady come to break the spell of winter gloom." She carried a basket topped with red-checked gingham.

"Hello, ma'am," she said to Jenny. "My husband, Edward, God bless him, come down with the rheumatiz; then he caught the chill a month ago and died just as the stage reached Eagle's Rock."

She seated herself on the trunk. "Folks said I'd find a squaw man and his family up here, so here I am, just in time for supper I see, thank goodness." Mrs. Mitten talked so fast that none of us had time to butt in.

"You must be the white girl from that unfortunate confrontation," she said to me. "But bless me, honey, you look like an Indian." If her smile hadn't seemed so friendly, I would have given her a shove.

"Carrie Hill," I said.

"And these darling half-breeds. Ma'am, you have beautiful children." Though I used to say the word *half-breed* without a thought, it now raised the hair on my neck to hear it. Breedin' was for cows or dogs, not people. But if it bothered them, they didn't show it.

"Since I invited myself, I brought a few things." She reached into her basket and unwrapped a blue cloth. Six gingerbread men with frosted hats and peppermint buttons. "Baked them myself this morning at an hour earlier than you've ever seen, children, on account of a cold bed and no husband t'warm it." She sat up straight and untied her bonnet. "But I won't burden you with my troubles. I am hungry as two horses. Now, how can I help?"

By the time Dick and Junior tramped in, we were more or less used to Mrs. Mitten. They didn't seem surprised to see a big woman leaning over our table, eating fast and eating lots.

"Heard good things about you, Beaver Dick,"

she said, before turning her attention back to her plate. She saw to the cleanup, and when the coffee had boiled she pulled a dark bottle out of her basket.

"To warm the insides." She poured generously into my cup and every other cup on the table. It burned going down, but did it ever feel good once it got there!

Mrs. Mitten kept calling us kids "honey" and telling funny adventures about Michigan before Edward came on the scene. Even Jenny laughed and moved herself onto Ingabumbee's knee.

Morning found me with the meanest headache and a stomach that wanted to turn inside out. Sometime after the party, Mrs. Mitten had strung a blanket across a corner of the room. Loud snoring was the only sign that she had survived.

When she finally sat up in her nightdress, she looked wobbly. Jenny kneeled beside her. She wasn't smiling.

"No more whiskey in my home." Then she loaded the stove for breakfast.

Mrs. Mitten stayed for two weeks. If she had more brown bottles in her basket, she didn't bring them out. Even though she did more than her share of chores, I kept thinking she might wear out her welcome. My aunt Ivy always fussed about company. "Guests and fish have one thing in common," she would complain. "After three days they stink."

But to Jenny, sharing seemed as natural as breathing. She wasn't worried that Mrs. Mitten might never leave or annoyed that she had arrived out of the blue. She was just THERE, eating and joking and brushing the children's hair. I liked her.

On Christmas Eve, Miles rode up with a scrub pine behind his horse and a little sack of carved soldiers tied to his saddle. Tom gave Jenny three snowrabbits ready for the pot. After dinner, Dick boiled molasses and butter for a taffy pull, then brought out his fiddle. Mrs. Mitten sang at the top of her lungs while William and Elisabeth danced an impromptu jig.

It was the first holiday without my family, and for a moment I wanted to close up and grieve. But the room was filled with so much cheer that the smells and sounds of Christmas weren't empty.

On the stroke of midnight, Miles twirled me in a waltz. As I looked into his eyes, I realized the feeling growing from the hole within me was nothing other than joy.

When Mrs. Mitten left on New Year's Day, the thermometer read thirty-seven degrees below zero. Inside, the windows were thick with ice, even though a fire roared from the stove. I had watched her dress that morning and figured if anybody would be warm, she would.

Over her pantaloons she pulled a corset cover cut from a bleached flour sack. It buttoned near the neck and at the waist but was open down the front. Then came two flannel petticoats, a factory petticoat, and a slip that hung from her shoulders to her knees. Over that she fastened a wool tweed skirt, and then another long slip. Finally, her big rustling dress, black. After she laced her boots over wool leggings, on went her cape and bonnet.

Jenny gave her a muff lined with rabbit fur. We could hear the sleigh bells for a long while after she left.

"I'll be back!" she called.

Soon it was warm enough for the children to play outside more often, although to my thin skin, nine degrees below zero did not seem warm at all. They ran in the snowshoes Jenny made for them from willow branches while I stumbled in mine. We dragged each other on scraps of hides and tried to roll balls into snowmen. Even with ice on the banks, Jenny would chip out a shallow pool to bathe in.

In the evenings Dick read aloud from a battered book he'd borrowed from Fort Hall. He told us Charles Dickens was the greatest author of the century and *Great Expectations* the most wonderful bunch of words we'd ever hear. Every few days, John sharpened my pencil with his knife so I could write in my journal. He did the same for his father.

By April the world dripped with spring. The once quiet river now creaked with melting ice, and the woods were noisy with the hammering of woodpeckers and the scolding of squirrels. Wildflowers pushed their way through patches of snow.

The May moon rose full and so bright that every twig cast a shadow. I tucked the children in, except for Junior, who was mending his moccasins by firelight. Jenny and Dick were outside.

When they came in later, the cabin was quiet. I was barely awake but I could hear them whispering. I knew they were moving together under their covers.

I wanted to look. How would I ever know about being a woman without Mother to tell me? And how would I learn to love a man like Jenny loved Ingabumbee?

Their sounds of pleasure grew louder. I closed my eyes and thought about Miles.

13

*"Little Dick caught a fine otter, me fixeng the packs
and saddels ... Jinny making a new lodge"*

6 July 1876

Summer meant we spent most of our time out-
doors. It was good to wear my cotton dress again
and sleep under the stars. Mosquitoes were our
only curse.

There was a cloud of dust in the distance, a
rider coming fast. And the only time folks around
here rode fast was when there was trouble with the
Indians or some kind of news—usually bad.

It was Jenny and me and the little ones that day.
When Beaver Dick had left at dawn, he had said
the next trip out would be all of us, so get ready.
We'd be packing east over the Teton range, down
into Jackson Hole.

"Good trappin's and the most beautifullest lakes you'll ever see," he had told me.

Now we watched the rider. Jenny had been showing me how to stitch canvas with the needles Dick traded for at Fort Hall. I kept a small chunk of wood in my palm so they wouldn't stab my skin. We'd been sewing wide strips to wide strips, and this morning I understood her purpose. There was enough canvas to cover a new stick tent.

In a faded way, it reminded me of Mother quilting with the ladies of Hannibal. A patch here and there, a sip of tea, and polite gossip helped them through their chore. I wondered what Mother would have thought to see me cross-legged in the dirt, my face darker than her parasol would have allowed.

The rider was getting closer, heading up the hill toward our cabin.

"Maybe he comes from Jim's," Jenny said. She stopped to watch with the rest of us. Jim Miller ran the cookhouse in Eagle's Rock, the town south of us, where travelers rested on their way to Pocatello Station.

"*Tsee-tsee,* come," she said to Elisabeth as she lifted her onto her hip. Jenny's face was calm, but I knew she was thinking. Whenever Beaver Dick was away, there was unspoken worry.

We could see the rider was Neal Benton, a wheezy little man with spectacles halfway down his nose and a derby propped on the tops of his ears. His legs flew out from the sides of his horse, almost lost in the dust as he rounded the knoll by the corral. Nothing was more important to Neal Benton than passing on a bit of news.

He was too winded to talk when he climbed down from his saddle. Junior took the reins and clicked his tongue as he led the mare in a cool-down walk.

"Miss Carrie?" he finally said, touching the brim of his hat. He didn't look at Jenny.

"I come to report a massacree of grave dimensions." He ran his tongue over his teeth, then spit a brown stream of tobacco juice into the dirt by Jenny's feet.

"General George Armstrong Custer was murdered in a savage attack near Little Bighorn River only days ago. Dead, ma'am, every last man of the Seventh Cavalry. Montana Territory ain't never gonna be the same."

Now he looked at Jenny. The sneer of his lip

was unmistakable. "Injuns," he said. "Them damned Injuns did it and got away scot-free."

My cheeks burned. Indians fighting, white men fighting, everybody fighting for something the other had. The way it was going, pretty soon we'd all kill each other, and no folks would be left to call themselves winners. I wasn't sure why, but I decided to glare at Neal Benton.

"Your friend, Mr. W. N. Shilling," he said to me, "he served under General Custer back in the Civil War. They was friends, I do believe. The dastardly news come by telegraph to the Pleasant Valley Station. Why, Lee Mantel is on the stage himself, headed to Fort Hall. Mr. Shilling is more'n likely hearing tears right this moment." He took his hat off, then greased his fingers through his hair.

"I'll have dinner, thank you, then be on my way."

The only problem with neighbors is having to be neighborly to rabble-rousers like Neal Benton. Jenny dished him up a bowl of stew and gave him a hunk of fry bread without looking at him. He squawked on like a magpie, wiping his sleeve across his mouth every minute or so. His unofficial job as reporter was something he took dead seriously.

"Other news few months back, on the fifth of March to be exact, Wild Bill Hickock married Miss Agnes Thatcher in Cheyenne. They's disappeared for parts north, trouble at their tails. I'll have some more of that bread, ma'am." He held his bowl toward Jenny. She didn't move.

When he saw he'd eaten up his welcome, he dropped his bowl on the ground for the dogs, then stood. As he was settling into his saddle, he looked right at Jenny.

"That General Custer, he was one powerful man. Mighta coulda been president if them savages would've know'd their place." His tongue moved to spit, but Junior stepped in front of his mother and cocked the Betsy.

Neal Benton pressed a handkerchief to his mouth. His neck was flushed red.

"He coulda been president," he tried again. I was ready to knock his yellow teeth out of his head; in fact, my fists were tight as hammers. Jenny looked into his eyes for the first time. She reached her hand toward his horse and stroked its long nose.

"Power does not make peace," she said softly.

Her eyes stayed on his. I wondered if he saw the circles of blue.

He kicked off into a gallop, his neck red as a sunset fading into the hills.

Unfortunately, that was not the last we'd see of him.

Part Two

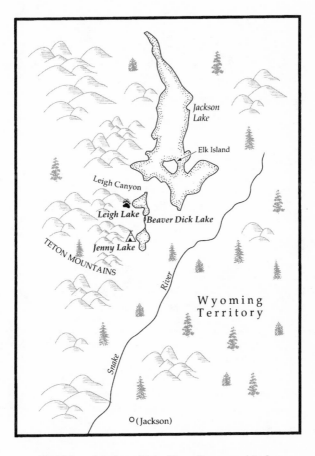

1876 Map of Jackson Hole, Teton Range, and Lakes

14

*"caught 2 beaver one of them ad got the chane [chain]
tangled in a bunch of willows while i was trying
to get him luce [loose] he made a plunge and got
his foot of [off] and got away...."*

21 July 1876

Elk scattered through the cottonwoods when we
reached Leigh's Creek. It was another four miles
upstream to the foot of the Tetons.

"Then it's near straight up over the range,
Missie," Dick said. I looked at our train. Nine
horses, four mules, and five young'uns with better
ideas for fun. Make that six. After a week on the
trail, we were complaining about camping out.

It was hot—too hot to be hoisting a tipi. But
that's what Jenny was doing while the little ones
played in the stream. She was moving more slowly
than usual; and when she rested her hand on her
stomach I noticed it was swollen.

I hurried to help with a pole. It was so tall it took both my arms to steady it against the others.

Her hand was still on her stomach. I was embarrassed, so I studied the coon tail flying from the top. The poles were always in the same perfect order, the door always opening to the sunrise.

Jenny must have noticed my look. "The child will come when the snows are deep," she said.

She started unfolding the canvas into a large half circle. Within an hour, the tent was up. I never heard her mention the baby again.

The days that followed formed a routine of work harder than any I'd ever seen. After breakfast Dick and Junior would ride ahead with a dozen or so traps clinking across the back of Gentleman Jack, the favored mule. We were to follow.

Jenny would break camp while Anne Jane, John, and I repacked the horses, using the diamond hitch Dick taught us.

Elisabeth and William sat in the travois behind Jenny, with the lodge poles. Carry-Me-Home now had her own saddle, which rode me a little higher in the throne; and thanks to the stirrups, I wasn't as tired at day's end. Branches scraped our legs as we trailed uphill, ducking boughs and trying to stay surefooted over fallen logs. We nooned just long enough to eat a bellyful of fat red raspberries, and then cup our hands in the stream.

Gnats swarmed around our eyes and mosquitoes bit through our clothes until we itched with welts. When Jenny could find wild mint, she crushed the leaves and rubbed them onto our skin. It was a small relief and often kept the bugs off until our night fires smoked them away.

Junior led us to the beaver swamps at the outlet of the Teton River. We stayed there until Dick had two minks, a muskrat, and a skunk. Just as he reached for a beaver struggling in a trap, it twisted its foot off and escaped. For supper we cooked John's string of trout and the two grouse Junior had whacked with his sling.

It was so hot, Jenny rolled up the bottom of the tent. We slept with a breeze, and a patch of starlight showing through the hole overhead.

In the morning, we were off again. Dick rode back to us, excited. We were on the border of Idaho and Wyoming.

"Two posts up ahead mark the line," he said. "We come through 'ere in '72 with 'Ayden and 'is surveying boys. Old Indian trail."

Jenny's mare, Bony, tripped in a badger hole and was limping so badly we unloaded her and left her by the creek. Next day, we camped in a grove of aspens, our feet aimed downhill so we wouldn't roll away in our sleep. After Dick pulled up the traps, he and Junior rode back for Bony. Soon we heard a shot ring through the trees.

"Put 'er out of 'er misery," he later explained. "Was on 'er knees in the water."

Rain soaked us the next six days. We rode barefoot, our moccasins rolled up dry inside the packs. John cut a trough in the dirt around the tent, and we closed up the top. All night long, thunder shook the earth, and we heard timber crack from a lightning strike.

By morning of the seventh day, the ground was loaded with currants and huckleberries knocked off their branches by the rain. We paused for an extra day, since the sun was hot and Jenny could dry the berries into patties.

The more I watched her and the children, the more I forgot about myself. We shared food, we shared beds, we laughed together. Every time Jenny spoke to me, a slight inflection in her voice made me feel as though she'd given me a great compliment.

Sometimes it seemed like Father was looking down on me and that Mother was listening from the trees. I knew they would be pleased.

The trail up was so narrow that the horses often slipped on loose shale. The sound of sliding rocks echoed in the canyon below. It was hot. One of the mosquito sores on my arm bled pus, and even through my sleeve the flies bit at it.

Anne Jane rode ahead of me. Suddenly the strap on her saddle snapped. Her horse stumbled with the shift in weight and began sliding over the edge, tail first. Anne Jane hung on to its neck.

"Mother," she cried. "Mama!"

But it was too late. Her horse rolled down the hill in a cloud of dust, over and over, its pack smashing open.

"Let go!" Dick yelled. He was on his feet, side-stepping in the shale. But Jenny was already ahead of him, deftly sliding on her side.

A pine stopped the horse long enough for Anne Jane to grab a branch. I watched with sadness as the horse hit the canyon bottom and rolled into the river. In a moment it was carried away.

A cut on Anne Jane's thigh spurted blood. Her ear was bleeding, too. Dick held her in his arms while Jenny bent over her. With one hand she leaned on the leg and with the other she pulled leaves from the brush next to her, then soaked them in her mouth. She pressed the wet leaves on the wound.

The little ones and I watched from the trail. It was almost dusk by the time Dick tucked Anne Jane in the travois and we found a bend wide enough to pitch our lodge. We stayed three days. Jenny didn't leave Anne Jane's side until color returned to her cheeks.

When we reached the plateau and could look down into Jackson Hole, I had to catch my breath. Above us towered the horns of the Tetons, snowy white even in July.

Below us, the lakes.

15

*"2 comarade trappers came along from Jacksons Lake . . .
thay report nothing to trap or hunt in that vercinaty
but Bair this seson and thay ware so plenty that it was
unsafe going the rounds to thare traps"*

8 August 1876

Dick pointed north. Wind whipped his hair around his face, which was red from the sun. I worried that my skirt would fill with air and sail me over the edge.

"Big one up there, Jackson's Lake," he said. He noticed Elisabeth at his feet and lifted her to his shoulders.

"Next, Leigh's Lake." John and Junior stood next to him, quiet as sentries. "Below it, see that little string of water? Well, sir, Mr. 'Ayden saw that in '72 and took kindly to namin' after yours truly. Beaver Dick Lake, that one is."

He laughed and ruffled William's hair. "Then, we got what I call the most beautifullest jewel in these parts, and don't you never forget it." He inhaled deeply.

"The one with blue like the clearest sky you ever seen. Well, when the gentleman surveyor met your mother, children, 'e named it after 'er. Tomorrow we'll 'ave our supper on the sunny side of Jenny's Lake." He lowered Elisabeth to the ground. "Yes, sir, we got the 'ole family in this valley."

As we descended through the canyon and the trail widened into a soft path of pine needles, I relaxed. It was peaceful and cool. Waterfalls spilling from the peaks filled the air with a distant roar. Sandhill cranes squawked in flight, the tips of their wings brushing the surface of the lake. An eagle flapped overhead. A large fish struggled in its claws. Soon the smell of wood smoke reached us from Jenny's fire, and we could hear the welcome sizzle of antelope steaks on the spit.

Morning brought two surprises. Long before dawn in the valley, the sun glowed from the summits above—a sight so splendid I stared in silence. Jenny waded in the lake, her face ready for the sun.

The other surprise was in a thicket not far from

our tent. It was the track of an animal so big that both my hands fit inside one paw print.

"Looks like Mr. Griz is fixin' t'dance," Dick said when William's yell brought him near.

"But don't look like 'e's too 'appy." He wiped his finger in the dirt. Blood. "You children make plenty of noise while you frisk about, eh?"

He swept his arm toward the lake and surrounding timber. "The Griz, they love this land as much as me and you. Open spaces and stands of pine." Dick swatted John playfully on his rump, then lifted William high.

"No boys 'untin' bears, y'ear? If y'don't sneak up on a Griz, it ain't gonna sneak up on you."

Junior stood by the lodge, his rifle across his arms. He was twelve now, and if he was afraid, he didn't show it.

By nightfall the bottoms of my feet were so bruised it hurt to walk. The children didn't mind wading shoeless, but to this greenhorn the pebbles were torture underfoot, even through my moccasins.

Jenny showed me how to hang them to dry, by fitting tips of fir branches inside. "They will be stiff after this sleep, but they will not shrink," she said.

But when I crept out of the tent at dawn, a

shawl around my shoulders against the chill, my moccasins were gone. I was looking under the tree when Dick cleared his throat.

"Either we got us a hungry mountain lion,"—he spit in his palms then rubbed them through his hair—"or Mr. Griz is watchin' us."

Before I could feel scared, a gunshot rang out. For a full minute we listened to its echo bouncing among the crags. Two figures on horseback were making their way toward us along the west shore. As there were no foothills, the riders were just dots at the base of the Tetons.

"It'll be 'igh noon 'fore they're shaking our 'ands. You might want Jenny t'stitch y'some new shoes, meantime." He turned me toward the lodge.

It was warm inside. The children still slept, small soft bumps of fur. Jenny was pushing twigs into the fire ring and blowing quietly on the coals. Soon a wisp of smoke curled to the top and out the opening. I stared up at the crisscross of poles, amazed at how easily the smoke found its way to the sky.

Jenny and I looked at each other. Her eyes held a calm that reached deep into me. The blue circles. We didn't need to speak.

16

*"i cooked and eate my dinner then took 3 traps
to set ... pased Jinny and childrn thay ware
diggeng away like good fellows"*

25 August 1876

Little Jimmy and John Reynolds looked like
they'd never been closer to civilization than a bear's
den. Both were missing teeth and their hair hung
to their shoulders in oily streaks.

Dick introduced them as old trapping buddies
from Yellowstone. After an hour of exchanging
howdies, they told a story that put an ache in my
heart.

We sat cross-legged on the shore, a fire of drift-
wood smoking out the mosquitoes. Jenny roasted
the ribs of two elk while several fish cooked on
sticks leaning toward the flames. The trappers

were describing their recent stay with a band of Crow Indians.

"We seen this girl sittin' by a squaw like they was siameeze twins." Little Jimmy gestured as if he were used to speaking in sign. His knees poked through his leggings. "This girl was a yellow hair, so I asks the old chief what's a yellow hair doin' s'far away from her own folks, and he tells me they traded her with some Assiniboins for some peace smokin'."

I sat up straight. A chill started behind my ears and shot down my spine. Questions flooded my mind, but I remained silent.

"Me 'n' Reynolds," he continued, "why, we offered t'buy her, so's she could go back t'her people. But she wouldn't budge, she wouldn't talk no English, and she keep hangin' on to that squaw, weepin' real pitiful for us to leave 'er be."

Mr. Reynolds unfolded a pouch of tobacco. With one hand he filled a square of paper; then he rolled it, lit it with a burning twig, and squinted. He seemed content to smoke and eye Jenny.

"We seen more. Cheyenne's got some little white kids; Nez Perce, too."

Little Jimmy helped himself to the nearest fish,

eating it hot off the stick. Juice dripped into his beard. "Near's we can tell, the Injuns treat most of 'em s'good, the kids ain't eager t'leave."

This made me think about my brothers.

When our wagon train arrived at Fort Hall, it was Mrs. Lander who told me my parents were dead. I asked her about Samuel, Joey, and baby Ivan.

"They're gone, too," was all she said.

Now I wondered. Before, I had just figured that Mrs. Lander meant they were dead. But she hadn't said that. A whole crop of hopes sprung up inside me, but I quickly pushed them down. There was no sense in letting trapper talk make me crazy with searching. The Hill brothers were gone, and that was that.

After Mr. Reynolds and Little Jimmy left for Teton Pass, we settled into the business of digging for yamps. We also found onions the size of musket balls, crisp and sweet, and we ate them while sitting in the grass.

The lake was always close, its water so clear that every pebble and rock was perfectly visible. The deeper I waded, the more the cold grabbed my legs. Here and there a submerged log lay mossy and quiet, a fish darting among its branches.

I looked ashore at Jenny. She was drying her hair in the sun. It fell below her waist, glossy black, the ends turning up in the breeze. When we stood next to each other, she was as tall as my shoulders, and she was now quite round.

Later, when William and Elisabeth curled into her lap to sleep, I leaned against the pine next to her. High above us the boughs swayed and sighed. I felt poetic.

"Jenny Lake doesn't do justice to your beauty," I whispered.

Snort. It sounded like a swallowed laugh.

"Your heart is big, Ohabumbee." She was laughing!

"Well, it's true."

"This water," she said slowly, "it is a gift from our creator. It does not need my name."

"But you're famous. People will remember you forever."

She stroked William's hair. "White men name these gifts after themselves. It is the *tybo* way to claim things that do not belong to them."

"But aren't you honored? Mr. Hayden must've really liked you."

"This lake is sacred to the Shoshoni people. We honor it for the great spirit of life." Jenny smiled. "To name such a thing for just one Indian..." She shook her head. "It is I who honor it."

She tipped her chin toward the Tetons. Dark clouds were settling over the snowy caps. Thunder rumbled in the distance. "Shoshoni call these Tee-winot, for the many peaks, you know. Ingabum-bee says the *tybo* have also named these peaks for themselves."

I remembered our wagons from Hannibal. Every time we had nooned or stopped for the night, one of us found a rock or tree to engrave. Some-where outside Springville was a pile of stones with "C. H. 1875" carved on top. My initials. We made monuments to prove our existence. We liked to change things if we could.

Jenny was different. Every time we broke camp, she was careful to undo the fire pit and spread its remains back into the ground. She filled holes from the tent stakes and she scattered bones for the wild animals. When we left, the campsite always looked exactly as it had when we'd first arrived: undisturbed. She simply wanted to pass through without a trace, like geese passing overhead on a southward flight.

I think I understood how she felt about her lake.

17

"rane with heavy thunder and lightning every 2 hours
thrue the night betwixt the storms the moon wold shine
out clere the heavy clouds comenced to rase to the top
of mount moran and the Big teton"

28 August 1876

Rain pattered on the tent all night. Inside we were
dry and warm. Smoke from the fire was heavy
around us but at least it discouraged the mosquitoes. Before dawn we were wakened by the noise
of a heavy animal running over the stony sandbar.
Dick and Jenny lifted their heads.

"Moose, maybe," he said reaching for the rifle.
Jenny sat up.

The noise came closer. Something big walked
slowly around the tipi. It was too dark to see, but
we could hear it sniffing us.

Fear pumped ice through me and I couldn't
move. Jenny clenched her knife. Dick eased the

113

gun to his chin and aimed it toward the sound. The children listened.

Then as quickly as the prowler came, it left. Dick lifted the flap slowly. We watched as a grizzly ambled across the stream to a tree where Dick had strung up a doe. The bear stood on its hind legs and with its front paws shook the trunk, swiping at the meat until its claws snagged it. Down it came on a bending branch.

"There goes our breakfast, folks," Dick said. "Watchdogs, Nig and Stumpy ain't. Where the bloody 'ell are those two?"

"Oppah, will the bear come back?" It was William.

"Why didn't you shoot the bear, Oppah?" asked John.

"Next time I see a grizzly, I'm gonna pop it right between the eyes," Junior said. He stood taller than Jenny, his boy arms crossed and his jaw set like no harm would ever touch her.

"See 'ere, young'uns." Dick looked out the tent again. "It's one thing t'kill a griz, but wounding it with your family in its path is quite another."

———

We moved camp up near Leigh's Lake. The streams feeding into it were icy clear and jumping with speckled trout. The boys made spears from peeled branches and did elaborate jumps and hoots while heaving the sticks into the water. All they got was wet.

Anne Jane and I sat on another bank with Elisabeth in my lap. We watched Jenny wade barelegged. For the longest time she stood motionless, then slowly lowered her arm into the water. A large fish was just inches from her hand, finning lazily in the current.

She eased her arm under its belly as smoothly as a leaf floating by. Suddenly there was a splash and up came Jenny's arm, her fingers hooked into the gills. She tossed the fish onto the grass, where it flopped in the sun.

When she screamed, I at first thought something in the water had bitten her. A huge shadow moving near us made me spin around and then I, too, started screaming.

18

*"there was a Grisly and hir cubs viseting my traps as
i went the rounds thay ad taken one beaver and
the trap with it in to the thick willows"*

10 September 1876

The bear stood taller than any man. It was a cabin's
width away. Panic rushed to my head and for a
moment I couldn't think.

"Carrie!" Anne Jane pulled my arm. She scooped
up Elisabeth and ran. I backed slowly into the
stream. Where did we leave the guns? My mind
was blank with fear.

Upriver came the shouts of the boys. Jenny
must have seen Anne Jane escape to safety, because she turned her attention to the other bank.
The guns.

"Hey-a, hey-a!" yelled Junior. He shoved John

116

and William into the brush and banged his sticks together.

With a terrible growl the bear began loping toward Jenny. She was almost to the guns.

"Hey-a!"

"Hey-a!" Junior and I shrieked together. The bear shook its massive head at the noise. Suddenly Nig and Stumpy leaped out of nowhere, barking furiously and snapping at the bear's hind legs.

I ran to Jenny. In an instant we both shouldered rifles. Without thinking and definitely without aiming, I fired. The bear roared then bit at its side. Jenny fired. Blood spurted from its neck. I fired again but only hit the dust at its feet.

Junior hurled his spear. It bounced off the grizzly's nose, distracting it long enough for the dogs to rip at its legs.

When I fired again, Mr. Bruin turned toward me, roaring with rage. I should have run, but it was fool's courage that made me shoot again.

I missed.

It came for me. A mass of brown fur, tips silver in the sunlight. I heard Jenny fire. Once.

Twice.

Again.

Blood spilled onto me from two holes in its chest. I stumbled, fell backward, then rolled just as the bear crashed to the ground. With one last desperate swipe, its claws raked my leg. Then it was still.

19

"the willows hanging over the little creek ad ice sickels a foot long dangling in the water it frose very hard last night we got so cold we ad to make fire 3 hours before daylight"

12 September 1876

It was several days before I could walk. Nig was wounded worse though, with half his side torn out. When Dick shot him, I felt I'd lost a friend.

Jenny changed the dressing on my leg often, pressing mud and white sage into the cuts, five long rows below my knee. Dick saw me rubbing mint around the scabs and said it was lucky my leg and I were still attached.

"Not many's get mauled by a griz and lives to show off a scar, Missie."

I wasn't planning to lift my skirts to show anyone, but it wouldn't take an eagle eye to notice I had a mighty limp. Sweet Sixteen and hobbling around like a great-grandma. What worried me more was my middle name: Sweet Sixteen and Never Been Kissed. Both Mother and Jenny had already had their first babies by the time they were my age, and I was not even close.

I leaned over a quiet pool at the edge of the lake. My reflection rippled under a breeze. It had been many weeks since I had stared at myself in Mother's looking glass. The scar on my forehead was gone.

I rather liked my tanned face and how my eyes were blue like Ingabumbee's and William's. It made it easier to feel part of the family. I copied Jenny, wearing my braids long and adorned with feathers or beaded leather. It was hard to imagine her as my mother, but it was a pleasant thought to consider myself her daughter.

As I debated my beauty, Jenny bathed in the cove beyond the sandbar. Her dress was drying on a sunny boulder. She was not concerned by her nakedness—not even by her stomach, huge with the child growing inside her. I envied her.

A shout, a splash, and there was Dick hooting beside her, naked as my birthday suit.

"Damnedest cold water this body's ever seen!"

Probably the *only* water his body's ever seen, I thought. He always smelled ripe, like his clothes just grew on him and stayed. His hands, neck, and face were as dark as Jenny's, but the rest of him was as white as a fish's belly.

He pressed himself gently to her back. She rolled her head so he could kiss her neck.

This time I didn't turn away.

When the days were too cool to sit in the shade, we packed up for home. With Bony and the other horse gone, we were down to seven horses, lonesome ol' Stumpy, and four mules loaded high with Dick's trappings. The nights were downright cold now, and in the mornings there was ice to break before we could drink.

Heading west through Leigh's Canyon was bumpy but easier traveling because of the crisp September air. Jenny walked most of the way although she was slow. Her saddle was filled with Elisabeth and the lump of folded bear fur.

Dick said Mr. Bruin must've weighed near nine hundred pounds, the biggest he'd ever seen in these parts. He saved its skull for Mr. C. H. Meriam, a collector back East. The claws he made into a necklace for Jenny. To kill a griz and live to wear it was the crown of the wilderness.

After Jenny pitched the tipi each afternoon, she cut pine boughs for the ground. I had never slept on a mattress so soft and so sweet smelling. Day by day the earth was freezing, but its cold didn't reach our sleeping bones.

When we dropped into the Teton Basin, the beaver swamps were dammed with ice. Dick's traps pulled up one fat beaver and two paws from getaways. Supper was roasted tail, a delicacy I knew none of my family had ever tasted. Dick lifted it off the coals with a branch then peeled off the steaming skin.

We followed Falls River to Henry's Fork, where in the distance a rider waved from his saddle.

"Halloo!" he shouted.

It was just the welcome party I wanted.

Part Three

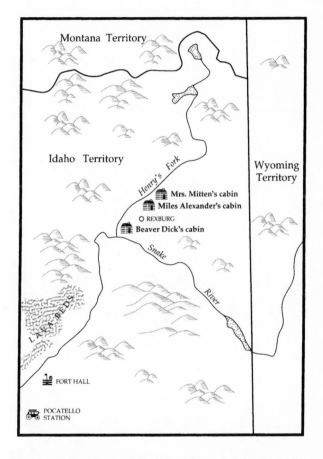

1876–78 Map of Henry's Fork Area, Jenny and Beaver Dick's Cabin, Miles Alexander's Cabin, and Mrs. Mitten's Cabin

20

*"Jinny made some good Butter the first time she ever
tryed she beat me all hallow"*

6 October 1876

Miles camped with us a day's ride from the cabin.
Only three months had passed since we last saw
each other, so I was unprepared for the flutter in
my heart. He was dark after a summer in the sun,
which made his eyes a paler blue. By the looks of
his ponytail, the barber must've bid farewell to Fort
Hall.

"You've come home at a good time, Carrie." We
sat outside after the others had turned in. The side
of the lodge glowed in the firelight, and the poles
cast spindly shadows onto the willows.

"Shirts need mendin' or something?"

He unrolled another blanket from his pack and

draped it over my shoulders. His face was inches from mine.

"Shirts nothin'. Don't think I could've stood another day missing you."

My neck felt hot. Surely he saw the blush spreading up to my cheeks. I didn't know what to say, so I studied the moon.

He placed his hand on my chin and moved slowly toward me.

"I thought about you day and night," he whispered. "Especially at night." Then he kissed me.

My heart beat fast. I closed my eyes and felt his hands tight around my waist; then he pulled back.

"Lordy, ma'am." He took a deep breath. "If I don't get you inside, Ingabumbee's gonna have a gun at my head tomorrow morning."

The cabin needed a good cleaning, for a family of raccoons had made themselves at home. Their tiny footprints tracked through what was left of the flour, and the sugar sack was ripped empty. The chimney had combed tufts of fur from their comings and goings, which made a mighty stink when Jenny lit the fire. I swept the floor with a willow branch.

While Dick and Tom Lavering drove a mule train to Fort Hall for supplies, Miles stayed nearby to help Junior hunt and stack wood. Every time I remembered our kiss, I felt all jumbly inside and wondered if it had been the same for Mother.

I now watched him carefully: the easy way he talked to Jenny, and the teasing he started with the children. For some odd reason, it was hard to talk around him. My words came out backwards, and what I did manage to say sounded silly. I'd catch him looking at me—a powerful strong look that made me go all soft.

Mother always used to tell me not to worry about falling in love.

"When you like someone, it will feel good," she had said one night while tying my hair up in rags. "But if it's love, darling, the pounding of your heart won't give you the quiet time to wonder."

I wished I could tell her what my heart spoke now.

On clear days the Tetons showed off their winter coats. Snow had dusted our valley, and once again we wore buckskins for warmth. Jenny started a new dress for me, but when I tried to wear it early, she laughed. The straight leather hem rubbed my skin raw. Without explaining, she kneeled at my feet with her knife. A few moments later my sleeves and hem were sliced into short fringe, soft as feathers.

In the midst of light snowfall, sleigh bells announced the arrival of Mrs. Mitten.

Howdies and hugs brought us up to date, as the stew simmered its ready smell. Jenny was unhurried, sometimes stopping to rest her hand on her side.

"And when I opened those jars of pumpkin, mercy, the stench." Mrs. Mitten was elbowed up at the table, Elisabeth in her ample lap. As usual no one butted in.

"You'd've had to be dead not to notice they were rotten. Anyway, I dumped the jars into the yard and hitched the buggy up for our ward meeting; took all day, that one did. Honey," she said to Anne Jane, "if you open m'basket, you'll find sweets for y'all." She buttered a square of johnny-cake for William.

"God as my witness, I never meant to hurt those chickens. But when I rode up in the evening, bless

me if they weren't all dead, every one of 'em, roos-
ter too, bellies plumped up with rotten pumpkin."

She winced, hand on her cheek. "Terrible sight,
was."

October splashed oranges and yellows onto the
aspens. The sky was noisy with geese honking
their way south. Dick returned with sacks of salt,
sugar, flour, and oats, sticks of peppermint, a Bible,
and another volume of Charles Dickens, *Bleak
House.*

Before Mrs. Mitten left, she baked a four-layer
chocolate cake to celebrate a happy event.

21

*"i comenced cuting house logs for winter quarters . . . lade
the foundaton 3 logs high of my cabben to day."*

10–11 October 1876

When Miles took my hand and, without a word,
led me past the corral, the afternoon sun was an
hour above the horizon. We stood on a knoll where
we could see the valley spread before us. In the distance, on either side, mountains rose up into white
peaks. There was no wind, only the chill air that
made frost as Miles spoke.

"Carrie Hill." He still held my hand. "My father
was a Philadelphia lawyer. I wish I had his gift for
oratory, but I don't."

I pulled my robe tighter and looked toward the
new shed Dick was building. Smoke wisped from
the cabin's chimney and from the stove's pipe. Jenny

and Mrs. Mitten would be laying supper by now, while the children wrestled with Stumpy. I was afraid to speak for fear the lump in my throat would catch my words again.

"It would make me the happiest man alive, Carrie, if you would say 'yes' when I ask you to marry me, which I just did." He laughed and threw his head back.

"Hoo-ie, that was easier than I thought." His eyes were so big and happy that I laughed, too. When I nodded, he let out a whoop and lifted me off my feet in a hug.

"Dang, I'm a lucky man!"

We stood there until the sun slipped behind the range, leaving a rosy cold sky.

The second kiss was much easier, and we took our time about it.

When we made our announcement, the children hooted and clapped, which set Stumpy to barking. Dick was there, shaking Miles's hand and smiling proud as a father. Mrs. Mitten held a hankie to her eyes.

"Dearie me, I love weddin's," she said between sniffs.

Jenny stood by the stove. We looked at each other in our quiet way, not needing to speak. Her dress fell in soft folds around her large middle, and tonight there were small shells tied into her braids. Then I did something I had never done before.

I rushed to put my arms around her.

Later that night, when the little ones were asleep and Miles was saddled for his cabin, Jenny brushed my hair with long, gentle strokes. "A Black Robe at Fort Hall married me and Ingabumbee," she said. "It was a happy day."

Dick looked up from his journal. He smiled at her.

"Yes, ma'am," he said. "The good Lord as our witness, it was."

We set the date for Christmas Eve, six weeks away. Meanwhile, I practiced my hand at the stove, and soon, thanks to Jenny, I had a specialty.

Into a pot of water I dropped six berry patties and boiled them until they were soft. Then a chunk of deer fat, a handful of flour, a few wild stirs, and in fifteen minutes, pudding! Soon, I had also filled a jug with chokecherry syrup for flapjacks. There was no telling what further miracles I would produce.

Winter continued to creep up. By November, the snow was knee-deep and hard going for the horses. The only path worth riding was the one along the frozen stream to Miles's and Tom's cabin.

We were forking hay to the stock the day Neal Benton delivered some chilling news. He arrived at a gallop, his horse breathing hard with icicles below its mouth. He didn't come near the cabin.

"Thought y'folks should know, there's Injuns all boiled up with the pox, down by Pocatello Station and Fort Hall," he said without dismounting. His horse stamped impatiently, then reared up. Benton reined it south.

"Dyin' like flies!" he yelled into the wind.

22

*"we were eating supper by the light of the camp
fire humpys Wife and Daughter 3 years old came
and sade humpy ad comited sueside and hur
and hir child were starving"*

11 November 1876

Two tipis were in sight around the bend. An Indian woman heavy with child came to the cabin with her little girl. Both were weeping. The husband had shot himself in the head an hour before, and in the other tent her parents lay dying.

Smallpox had come to Henry's Fork.

The woman didn't want to return to her camp, so Jenny began setting up her own lodge poles near the corral. Anne Jane and I hurried to help her, while Junior unfolded the canvas and extra robes. Jenny packed a basket of food, but Dick begged her not to go near.

"She might 'ave touched the pox. Just leave the food at the lodge door." He took her hands. "Please, Jenny."

"Her time is near, Ingabumbee. If she needs me, then I will go."

Miles and Tom rode upstream. The old people were dead. Soon we could see flames from the burning tipis. A terrible fear made me go cold inside.

Would we be next? My mind raced back to my childhood. I remembered Father vaccinating us, but for which disease, I didn't know. Cowpox sounded familiar, but was it the same as smallpox?

Jenny laid breakfast and supper outside the tipi. The woman often wandered off with her daughter. Her wail reached us on the wind.

Everything else seemed normal. Jenny finished the beadwork on a tiny new cradleboard. Dick and Junior hunted rabbits. Anne Jane and I broke ice for water. Miles was there every day but we didn't talk about our plans. Christmas Eve seemed very far off now.

———

Early one morning we jumped awake to a woman's scream. Jenny was the first one out the door, her robe a dark blur in the blowing snow.

"You young'uns stay'ere," Dick ordered. He pulled on his coat and waited out by the corral.

23

*"i told him to tell tex [Texas Barker] if that womon
came to his place to send hur off for we suspected
she ad beene were the small pox was"*

12 November 1876

The hours were slow. Dick hollered to Jenny, but she didn't come out. He returned to the cabin.

By evening, snow had buried the woodpile. All we could see of the tipi were its dark poles pointed toward the heavens. I wondered when Jenny's own child would be born.

Supper was quiet. Occasionally Miles and I brushed against each other as we moved about the cabin. Finally Dick slammed his mug on the table.

"By God, what we need is some fiddlin'. Tom," he directed, "your 'monica is on the sill over there. Miles, I do believe y'can blow a jug."

He lifted his foot to a stool, waved his bow into

position, and began sawing the strings. "And away we go!"

Immediately the mood lifted, and the children started giggling. They stomped like cloggers at a fair, arms swinging and shoving each other. Several minutes of this dimmed my thoughts about the snow outside and the dark tipi.

But when the door opened, our music stopped. Jenny held the little girl's hand, and in her other arm was a bundle of fur. By the looks of Jenny's face, we knew the mother was dead.

"Well, sweet'eart," Dick said quickly, bending down to the child, "looks like you 'ave a new baby sister or brother, eh?" His eyes were a question mark to Jenny.

"Sister," she said without expression.

A pot of water on the stove was hot. Jenny handed the sleeping infant to me as she filled a bucket mixed with snow.

As Jenny bathed her, the baby threw her tiny arms wide with surprise and screwed up her face for a loud cry. We crowded around. The scene reminded me of the morning Ivan was born. But his tub had been of white porcelain, his blankets edged with lace, and his skin didn't have all the little flea bites that covered this baby.

"Jenny," Dick said softly. "Was there spots on the woman?"

She shook her head. "No."

We considered the other child. I smiled when I recognized Shy One. She and Grandmother Humpy had made me feel so welcome all those months ago. Where was the old woman now? I wondered.

A warm bath revealed no spots on Shy One, and there was unspoken relief. Jenny later sewed a blanket around the mother and left her in the tipi. Miles and Dick surrounded its base with rocks to keep animals out.

Shy One played with the children as if nothing had happened. Maybe because she was so instantly adopted by all of us, she didn't realize she was orphaned. Jenny nursed the infant at her own breast, after diapering her with a soft strip of sagebrush bark.

The next morning, I woke before dawn. The cabin was strangely quiet.

I looked out the window to see Jenny walking

toward the tipi, something small cradled in her arms.

Shy One stared through oozy eyes. Her face and neck were so swollen with boils, she had trouble swallowing. I didn't know what to do. I remembered the Indian doll she'd given me and quickly found it. She seemed happy to see it again but still didn't want to sit up. I changed her bedding.

For the next three days, Shy One lay hot with fever or wet with chills and diarrhea. When she died, Dick carried her out to her mother and sister. The tipi burned quickly in the dry air.

24

*"the dogs run some deer out and i Kiled one of them
wile i was dressing it i looked a cros the creek and saw
some one with tom thay was a long ways from me
but something told me it was my son Richard [Junior]
and that thare was somthing rong at home"*

14 December 1876

The cold worked its way into your bones unless you
stayed smack in front of the stove. The rows on my
leg ached constantly. My fingers would freeze on
the pail handle, and it took several minutes in the
cabin before I could uncurl them. Once Elisabeth
followed Junior to the shed. When he heard a
muffled cry, he saw she'd stuck her tongue onto a
metal harness to taste the salt. Dick poured a cup
of hot coffee down her cheek to melt the ice, but
her tongue still lost a layer of skin.

Two weeks before Christmas, Anne Jane woke
up moaning. Her head hurt, she said, and her
back. She was shivering, so Jenny piled on extra

blankets and sat with her. Dick left with Miles to hunt. We all needed new moccasins.

When Jenny doubled over near the hearth, I yelled at Junior to run for help. The baby was coming.

All night and the next day she lay in bed, sometimes moving herself closer to the fire or to check on Anne Jane and Elisabeth, who also was fevered. Something seemed wrong. I was frightened.

"Ingabumbee," Jenny whispered. Dick sat behind her to support her back. Her knees were up, and with a loud gasp she reached between her legs. I saw she was touching a small head; then, with another deep breath, her face squeezed tight and the baby was out.

She held it to her, a perfectly formed little girl with a mop of dark wet hair. It didn't make a sound. It didn't move. A few moments later, Dick took the infant while Jenny bit the cord off.

I watched as he wrapped her in a square of fur and laced her into the cradleboard. The baby's eyes were closed, her skin bluish gray. Without a word Dick covered her face. Jenny lay on her side.

For the next two days, the children slept fitfully,

crying out, asking for blankets, only to kick them off minutes later. I felt sick inside from the panic that grew by the hour. William's mouth was swollen with boils, and every time I put a cup to his lips he screamed.

"What can we do?" I cried to Dick.

His look filled me with despair. Ingabumbee was ill, too.

He fastened on his cape and carried kindling outside. After he knocked the snow off a sagebrush he torched its branches. The bonfire brought Miles and Tom within an hour.

Jenny moved in and out of sleep. Like the children, she breathed with a rattling sound, and she could not eat. The smallest sips of water gave her the flux, and soon she was too weak to crawl for the bucket.

Dick wouldn't leave her side, though he, too, often fainted. His neck was covered with pustules the size of buttons. He read to her from the *Harper's Magazine,* and she would try to smile at its bright pictures.

"You're gonna be just fine, Jenny," he kept saying to her. "You'll see."

Tom and I exhausted ourselves tending the little

ones, washing their soiled clothes and trying to keep their beds dry. We tied their hands with rags to keep them from scratching. The room had the rancid smell of wet goose feathers. Miles kept feeding wood into the stove. Nights were long, with most of us awake.

Then finally Jenny sat up. Her face was serene as Dick held her.

"Children," she started. Then she lay her head in his arm and closed her eyes.

"Jenny?" He shook her gently. "Oh, God," he wailed.

Miles and I stared at each other in disbelief. Jenny dead? It couldn't be. My head felt pinched. I searched Miles's face for comfort, but it was twisted with anger.

He pressed his fingers over his eyes and swallowed hard. "Maybe we can save the others, Carrie. This is the *tybo*'s sickness, dammit, *tybos* should do something to help."

He dressed in furs, his eyes on the sleeping children. "I'll bring back Dr. Fuller from the reservation, soon as I can." He kissed my cheek.

"God keep you, Carrie."

Fort Hall was three days away, maybe more through the snow. As I watched him go, tears filled my eyes. He passed under the cottonwood branch where Dick had strapped the cradleboard and where Jenny's baby lay like a sleeping flower.

25

"my hart was ded within me"

December 1876

Dick wrapped Jenny in a blanket and a buffalo robe after dressing her in her beaded buckskins. Tom helped carry her out to the wagon; then they put Sleeping Flower next to her. It was snowing again—huge flakes the size of my thumbnail.

Tom rested his hand on Dick's shoulder. "It'll take you a year to dig through this ice, old man."

I pulled my blanket across my mouth. Frost puffed in front of their beards as they looked at each other.

"Your woodpile there." Tom stretched his arm toward the north side of the cabin. "Won't take but a minute for me and you to stack them logs

148

around the end, corral-like. Keep varmits out. Come spring, we'll dig where you want." He wiped his sleeve across his nose and coughed.

Dick leaned over the wagon and buried his face in Jenny's robe. His hand pulled Sleeping Flower closer to her mother. Then he turned toward the logs.

The fire had gone out. I loaded the stove with chunks of kindling and blew the coals into flame. Junior rolled onto his side to watch.

"Is my mother in Heaven now, Carrie?" he whispered. "God bless my poor mother."

I covered him and put my lips to his forehead. He was hot. The thumping of logs against the wall outside shook the beds, but the children slept on.

"Missie?" Dick was huddled by the fire, Anne Jane under one arm, and Elisabeth in the other. Their faces were so puffy with red sores, they looked like strangers.

I kneeled at their feet.

"If you're not feelin' poorly, could y'make it to the fat lady's? She might 'ave some patent med'cins to 'elp."

"I want to stay with you and the children."

"But if y'can beat that rez doctor . . ." He closed his eyes.

Mrs. Mitten's place was at least a day's ride. Providing it didn't storm, I could be back by Christmas Eve.

"I'll go, Ingabumbee."

26

i cannot discribe my felings or situaton at this time i knew i must ave sleep but could not ... sleep so i got up and adminestrad to my famley a gane with the ditermaton [determination] to doing all i could until i died witch i was sure i could not [last] more than 24 hours longer for my eyes would get full of black spots and near blind me and death would ave beene welcome only for my children i saw the spots go back on William and ann Jane my oldist daughter to day ...

this night i felt some sines of sleep but with the sine came a heavy sweting and burning and tremors ... my close [clothes] and the beding was ringeng wet in half an hour i told tom . . . to save some of my famely if it was posable and turned over to die i can not write one hundreth part that pased thrue my mind at this time as i thaught deth was on me

i sade Jinny i will sone be with you and fell a sleep

tom sade i ad beene a sleep a half hour when i woke up every thing was wet with prespeaton i was very weak i lade for 10 or 15 minuts and saw William and ann Jane ad to be taken up to ease them selves every 5 minutes and Dick Juner very unrestlas [restless] i could not bare to see it

i got up and went to elp tom . . . i saw that the spots ad gone back on Dick my Detirmaton was to stand by them and die with them this was cristmos eve

Ann Jane died about 8 Oclock about the time every year i used to give them a candy puling and thay menchond about the candy puling meny times wile sick espeshely my son John

Willian died on the 25 about 9 or 10 Oclock in the evening

John and Elisabath was doing well thay was a head of the rest in the desise [disease] the scab was out and dryeng up on the night of the 26th . . . tom was taken with dyaria 2 days ago and was to weak to get up to asist us eny more *on the 26th Dick Juner died betwixt 5 and 6 oclock in the evening*

last night when i woke up the fire was out but some small coles the lamp burned down and the dore of the cabin partly open i was fresing [freezing]...

my son John had comenced to swell agane about day light and about 8 oclock on the 27 in the eveng he died

[that] night...i woke up cold a gane [again]... after sleeping 5 or 6 hours...i got up as quick as my strength wold let me

[Elisabeth] caught cold and sweled up a gane and died on the 28 of Dec abot 2 Oclock in the morning this was the hardest blow of all

i was taken with the Bludy flucks [flux] this night and me and tom layed betwixt life and death for severl days...

I ad not slept more then [than] 2 hours and that was a misroble [miserable] swet and tremor sleep for the last 13 days...i did not expect to live...but god as spard me for some work or other i believe and i am prepard to do it what ever it is

[I'm] ready to move to my place at the elbo of the tetohn i shall improve the place and live and die near my famley but i shall not be able to do eny thing for a

few months for my mind is disturbed at the sight that i see around me and [the] work that my famley as done wile thay were liveng the meny little presants you ave sent to me and famley i shall keep in memory of you and them

from a letter Beaver Dick wrote to Dr. Josiah Curtis, his friend and one of the hunters he had guided into Jackson Hole

27

"the antlope comes and looks in to my little vally nearly every day i don't kill eny dont want to no one to eate the meat and i cannot waste with a good conshus [conscience]"

6 May 1878

By the time Carry-Me-Home and I reached Mrs. Mitten's place, a wind from the north was blowing snow sideways like needles of ice. The blizzard lasted nine days. Drifts were high as the roof, and it took us another day to dig a path to the barn.

Miles met us before we sighted Ingabumbee's cabin. I was overjoyed to see that Miles was safe, but stricken with silence at his news.

I remembered Father once consoling a widow after he tried to save her husband. Something about God's plan and how we all have a special

purpose in life. Being called home was how he explained death. But his words were no comfort to
me now. Maybe fairness was something only the
Creator understood.

Mrs. Mitten took me under her wing, but I was
not the lively companion of old. For many weeks I
ached with sorrow. I missed Jenny. I missed her
little ones.

Then one morning, when a warm breeze brought
the song of a robin, I felt Jenny was near. She
wouldn't have wanted me to grieve. *Care for the
ones who live* is what she would say. *Care for life.*

Miles and I were married when the wildflowers
bloomed. Dick and Mrs. Mitten were with us;
Tom, too, and John Hogue. We built our home
near Henry's south fork, as easy ride to the new
little town folks were calling Rexburg.

When I told Miles we were going to have a
baby, he carried me to the top of our small hill,
where the grasses waved yellow in the wind. He
turned his face to the sun. Finally he opened his
eyes and looked at me.

His cheeks were wet.

———

It was an open winter with almost no snow. On the balmy night of February 27, 1878, I gave birth to a plump, squalling little girl. Mrs. Mitten talked me through the long hours of labor, and Miles was there, sleeves rolled up, to first hold our daughter, Jenny Jane Alexander.

28

*"oh i wosh [wish] i could give to the world my experance
in indian life and the rocky mountins so thay could
understand it but i lack educaton to do it myself"*

12 September 1878

At dusk I was surprised to see Beaver Dick
out by the garden talking to Miles. We hadn't seen
him for months. I put another plate on the table.

When they came in, Miles slid his arm around
my shoulder.

"Ingabumbee has a story I think you should listen to, honey."

Jenny Jane slept in her box by the door. Summer
heat stayed in the room like an unwelcome guest.

"Their lodges were outside Pocatello Station.
We talked late into the night." Dick paused long
enough to eat a chunk of corn bread, every last

crumb. I tried to ignore the pox scars that covered his neck.

"Next morning was when I thought this old trapper 'ad lost 'is mind." His head bent over his stew, but his eyes looked up at me. "Missie, I swear I saw our William, sitting next to an old squaw."

"But William ..." is dead, I wanted to say.

"A blue-eyed *ohabumbee,* quiet as a rock."

Miles took my hand.

"Shoshoni found 'im near dead at Raft River, hiding under a cave of willows. Signs of Blackfeet everywhere. Lord, Missie, 'ow you've learned to cook," he said. He held his plate for seconds.

I hadn't touched mine.

"They call the boy Broken Wing because of 'is arm. When I spoke English to 'im 'e looked to cry. 'Is words were scratchy. Couldn't tell me 'is name, Missie," he stopped to swallow and wipe his beard with his sleeve. "But Broken Wing was finally able to say 'is father 'ad been a *tybo* medicine man."

My throat squeezed tight. I could feel my heart pounding under my shirt. Miles kept his hand over mine.

"Them Shoshoni is on their way; should be 'ere in a few days."

Miles thought a moment. "When did they find Broken Wing?"

Dick tipped his chair back and picked his teeth with his fingernail. "That's the other thing you should know, Missie. Spotted Eagle said seven moons ago. Before the snows. No telling 'ow long 'e'd been with the Blackfeet before that."

Part of me wanted to lie down and sleep, to hide this news. But part of me stirred awake with a hope I thought had died.

"But 'e's dark as a breed," Dick continued, "with a yellow braid down 'is back. Since I ain't never seen white folks dress their boys like that, it'd be my guess 'e's been with Indians three, maybe four years."

Three, maybe four years. My mind raced back to the ambush. Had it been that long? A doctor's child captured by a raiding party. Could it be?

The next days were torture. I wanted to jump on Carry-Me-Home and hurry south. Who was this white boy? Every moment of every day I busied myself like a hen before the storm. Nights I lay awake. Jenny Jane was a blur of a baby at my breast.

Then the horizon moved: a dozen Shoshoni on horseback, several pulling travois. Dick rode out to them, and soon they were headed toward the cabin.

I ran. A sob caught in my chest when I saw him. He was high on a pinto, a rough little boy dressed like an Indian. But there was no mistaking the doctor's son, my brother Joey.

He stared at me, blue eyes water. He looked over at the old woman on the horse beside him. I recognized Grandmother Humpy. She nodded.

Then he was in my arms. When I opened my eyes again, the smile of an old grandmother was upon us.

Epilogue

Jenny Leigh died on December 18, 1876. She was twenty-seven years old.

Today her grave and those of her children can be seen on a grassy bank of Henry's Fork near Rexburg, Idaho, a few hundred yards from where their cabin stood.

When Beaver Dick recovered from the smallpox, he burned their home to the ground and in March moved north to the ranch he and Jenny had built on an elbow of the Teton River. His health was never as robust as before, and he never again celebrated Christmas or New Year's. He continued to guide parties of prominent and wealthy sportsmen from the East into Jackson Hole, among them Thomas Moran in 1879, Theodore Roosevelt in

1892, and Louie Vanderbilt. Some of Dick's hunting specimens are still on display at the Smithsonian Institution in Washington, D.C.

When he was about fifty, he married Sue Tadpole, a fourteen-year-old Bannock Indian, who bore them three children—Emma, William, and Rose.

Glossary of Shoshoni Words

ingabumbee—red hair

goh-no—cradleboard

nabia-tsee—my dear mother

ohabumbee—yellow hair

oppah—father

teewinot—many peaks

tsee-tsee—darling; papoose

tybo—white person

Shoshone refers to the tribe; *Shoshoni* refers to both the language and the plural.

Bibliography

Betts, Robert B. *Along the Ramparts of the Tetons.* Boulder, Colo.: Associated University Press (1978).

Conley, Cort. *Idaho for the Curious: A Guide.* Cambridge, Idaho: Backeddy Books (1982).

DeVoto, Bernard, ed. *The Journals of Lewis and Clark.* Boston: Houghton Mifflin (1953).

Fryxell, Fritiof. *Campfire Tales of Jackson Hole.* Moose, Wyo.: Grand Teton Natural History Association (1969).

Huidekoper, Virginia. *The Early Days in Jackson Hole.* Boulder, Colo.: Colorado Associate University Press (1978).

Leigh, Richard. "Writings of Richard 'Beaver Dick' Leigh: a collection of his original diaries and letters." Laramie, Wyo.: Western History Research Center, University of Wyoming.

Ruxton, George Frederick. *Life in the Far West.* London (1849).

Schreier, Carl. *Grand Teton Explorers Guide.* Moose, Wyo.: Homestead Publications (1982).

Swetnam, Susan, comp. "Southeast Idaho Family and Place Histories." Pocatello, Idaho: Idaho State University Archives.

Thompson, Edith M. Shultz, and William Leigh Thompson. *Beaver Dick: The Honor and the Heartbreak: An Historical Biography of Richard (Beaver Dick) Leigh.* Laramie, Wyo.: Jelm Mountain Press (1982).

Kristiana Gregory began writing stories when she was eight years old. During summer camping trips in the mountains of New Mexico, her parents taught her to respect the environment and to feel at peace with nature. She wrote *Jenny of the Tetons* to honor the memory of Jenny Leigh, a woman who "symbolizes other women and other American Indians who have been lost to history." Ms. Gregory has worked as a reporter, an editor, and a children's book reviewer. She lives with her family in Redlands, California.

Kristiana Gregory's adventures of a white boy adopted as the son of a Shoshoni chief's mother

The Legend of Jimmy Spoon

Not all Shoshoni tribes are pleased that a white boy lives among them....

A tall Indian had just snared a rabbit and was mounting his horse. Yes, he had seen Jimmy's horse, Pinto Bean. He pulled Jimmy into the saddle behind him.

"We will find your pony."

Suddenly the rider kicked into a gallop, his legs flying out from the horse's sides. Jimmy was terrified.

"Stop, please!" he cried.

Jimmy didn't want to be captured by White Plume. He tried to think. The only way to escape was to jump, but the horse was moving too fast. It was also much taller than Pinto Bean; it would be a long fall to the ground.

But jumping was his only chance. He waited. A grove of aspen was up ahead. It came closer.

The horse began to slow down among the trees.

Jimmy reached up with both hands.

Now!

He grabbed a low branch. The instant he did, his body jerked out of the saddle. He crashed onto the trail and scrambled as fast as he could toward camp, glancing over his shoulder.

The Indian had already reined his horse around and was in a fierce gallop, lasso twirling in the air.

The rope landed over Jimmy's neck and under one arm, dragging him several yards. The man hit him with his quirt. Jimmy lay in the dirt, stunned.

**Kristiana Gregory dramatizes the
catastrophic San Francisco earthquake
with shattering immediacy**

Earthquake (at Dawn

An ALA Best Book for Young Adults

*A New York Public Library Book
for the Teen Age*

*An NCSS-CBC Notable Children's Trade Book
in the Field of Social Studies*

Photographer Edith Irvine and her maid, fifteen-year-old Daisy Valentine, are en route to a photography exhibit in Europe when their travels are abruptly canceled. From a boat in the harbor, Edith, her father, and Daisy watch the San Francisco shoreline in horror. . . .

Something thumped our boat. Edith and I grabbed the rail. Mr. Irvine hugged Edith protectively and looked beyond the bow.

"See anything?" the captain called to his crew.

Before anyone could answer, we heard an ear-splitting boom, as if ten cannons had exploded. All heads turned toward shore. Immediately every light blacked out, darkening the city into a silhouette against the lightening sky.

"Papa, what's happened?"

A women next to us screamed, then someone cried out the horrible word:

"Earthquake!"

Have you read these Great Episodes?

SHERRY GARLAND
In the Shadow of the Alamo
Indio

KRISTIANA GREGORY
Earthquake at Dawn
The Legend of Jimmy Spoon

LEN HILTS
Quanah Parker: Warrior for Freedom,
Ambassador for Peace

DOROTHEA JENSEN
The Riddle of Penncroft Farm

JACKIE FRENCH KOLLER
The Primrose Way

CAROLYN MEYER
Where the Broken Heart Still Beats:
The Story of Cynthia Ann Parker

SEYMOUR REIT
Behind Rebel Lines: The Incredible
Story of Emma Edmonds, Civil War Spy
Guns for General Washington:
A Story of the American Revolution

ANN RINALDI

An Acquaintance with Darkness

A Break with Charity:
A Story about the Salem Witch Trials

Cast Two Shadows:
The American Revolution in the South

The Coffin Quilt: The Feud between
the Hatfields and the McCoys

The Fifth of March:
A Story of the Boston Massacre

Finishing Becca: A Story about
Peggy Shippen and Benedict Arnold

Hang a Thousand Trees with Ribbons:
The Story of Phillis Wheatley

A Ride into Morning:
The Story of Tempe Wick

The Secret of Sarah Revere

The Staircase

ROLAND SMITH

The Captain's Dog: My Journey
with the Lewis and Clark Tribe

THEODORE TAYLOR

Air Raid—Pearl Harbor!
The Story of December 7, 1941

The Spookiest Pumpkin

by Andy Rector

Illustrated by
Yacoba

Spider sat in the pumpkin patch. She could tell the pumpkins were excited about something. But what could it be?

Spider crawled over to a pumpkin who sat at the edge of the patch. "Hello. What is your name?"

The pumpkin said, "My name is Jacko."

"I'm Spider," Spider said. "You're a big, big, big pumpkin."

"Maybe to you I am big," said Jacko. "But see how small I am compared to the other pumpkins?"

Spider looked around the pumpkin patch. It was true. All the other pumpkins...

were taller or wider...

or brighter or rounder than
Jacko.

"They will all get picked for Halloween," said Jacko. "They will get to be jack-o-lanterns. I will be left out here in the pumpkin patch by myself. I'm just too small."

Spider said, "You seem like a wonderful pumpkin to me. Someone will surely pick you for Halloween."

"I doubt it!" said a loud voice. Spider jumped.

"Who said that?" she asked.

Spider saw a tall pumpkin looking at them.

"I did," said the tall pumpkin. "He's too short!"

"He's too narrow," said a wide pumpkin.

"He's too dull," said a bright pumpkin.

"He's too flat," said a round pumpkin.

All the pumpkins in the patch laughed at Jacko.

Jacko looked sad.

"Don't listen to them," said Spider. "I'll be your friend."

Spider stayed with Jacko that night.

The next morning, a noise woke Spider. She heard the voices of children! They were picking out pumpkins.

"Oh I hope I get picked," said Jacko. "I want to be a Jack-o-lantern."

All the other pumpkins got picked. But no one picked Jacko. Spider felt sad because Jacko felt sad.

"Maybe this will cheer you up," said Spider. Jacko could see Spider beginning to spin some-thing. Soon she decorated Jacko with her webs.

"This is my home now," said Spider. "I'll stay with you."

And she did until . . .

The day before Halloween, some of the children came back.

"We need one more pumpkin," said the girl.

"But we picked all of them the other day," said the boy.

"Oh, look," said the girl. "The only pumpkin left is that little one. See it?"

"Wow," said the boy. "It looks spooky with all those spider webs on it."

"It's perfect!" they said.

Jacko may not have been the tallest, or widest, or brightest, or roundest Jack-o-lantern at the party, but—thanks to Spider's webs—he was the spookiest.